# SURVIVAL IN A NIGHTMARE

The scenery was phenomenal. Sheer canyon walls loomed, seeming taller than they were because mist shrouded the upper reaches...The fungus and mildew and moss had now multiplied fantastically...Zena did not know whether the nutrients in the alien water had fertilized this explosive growth, or whether the plant growth thrived on sediments from the catastrophic erosion, but thrive it did. The stuff was slippery when squashed, so that she was always afraid of falling. It had a vile smell when bruised.

Zena lifted her head with a startled notion. "The moss—if we could eat *that*—"

# PIERS ANTHONY

# RINGS OF ICE

### With a Terminal Essay
### by Donald L. Cyr

AVON BOOKS ◆ NEW YORK

AVON BOOKS
A division of
The Hearst Corporation
105 Madison Avenue
New York, New York 10016

First Avon Printing: June 1974

AVON TRADEMARK REG. U.S. PAT. OFF. AND IN OTHER COUNTRIES, MARCA REGISTRADA, HECHO EN U.S.A.

Printed in the U.S.A.

K-R 10 9 8 7 6 5

# RINGS OF ICE

# Chapter 1: Rain

Noon—but the depth of swirling cloud blanked out any suggestion of the sun and made the air chill. She stood forlornly on the approach to the Interstate highway, knowing the chances were fifty-fifty that any car that stopped for her would mean trouble for a lone young woman. But trouble or no, she had to get a ride; time was running out.

She saw the small bus as the first fat drops of rain slanted down. The vehicle was moving slowly around the loop of the approach, feeling its way. There was no reason to assume it was slowing for her.

She forced her eyes off it, watching the rain smash into the dry dirt embankment beyond the road. The huge drops actually excavated little craters. Meteorologically, she knew, this was known as rain-drop blast, and it could be a substantial if little-known source of erosion. The construction company should either have paved the embankment or seeded it with grass. Perhaps that had been scheduled for next week. As it stood, a few good storms would carry down so much earth that the job would soon have to be done over.

In fact, one good storm would wash it out. This one. Not that it mattered. The world as she knew it was coming to an end.

The downpour developed so rapidly that by the time the bus pulled abreast of her she was drenched. But the vehicle stopped, it stopped!

It was not a bus after all, or a van, but a motorized trailer, a camper, a motor home. There was a massive "W" on its side, with a painted line trailing all the way to the rear. Winnebago—she had seen them on the road before, but never been inside one. Its door was set back a few feet, in the side, and it had bus-like windows. Privately owned—and surely by a wealthy family. Well, any port in a storm—especially *this* storm!

The door opened. She climbed in. Her wet skirt caught at her thighs, making the ascent awkward, and she was dripping water all over the fine shag carpeting inside.

A handsome, hearty man stopped looking at her legs long enough to give her a hand up. She stiffened, but reminded herself that she was the one begging the favor of a ride. It ill behooved her to antagonize anyone at the outset.

"Hi!" the big man said. "I'm Gus Gunter." He gestured to his companion, the driver. "This is Thatch. Thatcher Zane. You?"

"Zena Emers," she said, looking about. The interior was elegant—an amazing contrast to the stark metal exterior. There was a dinette opposite the entrance, with a map of North America set into the plastic table surface. The upholstery was in dark leatherette, looking expensive and new. The carpeting extended all the way down the central hall to the back.

8

It was not the sudden luxury that dismayed her so much as the human situation. With every vestige of her clothing plastered against her body, she was suddenly thrust into a traveling bachelor apartment. Maybe she would be better off in the rain.

"Get it moving, Thatch," Gus said. Had he read her mind?

The driver shook his head dubiously. He was a medium-small man with heavy-lensed glasses that distorted his pale brown eyes, and he had a moderately receding chin. His face was scarred as if by smallpox or childhood acne. His hairline was drawing back from his forehead, though he could not be over thirty. As men went, wholly unimpressive.

"I don't know," Thatch muttered. "She's all wet, and the visibility—" His voice was somewhat nasal, in contrast to the chesty timbre of his handsome friend.

"You worrying about the visibility outside—or inside?" Gus demanded. It might have been a joke, but he wasn't smiling, and Zena herself was all too well aware of her involuntary exposure. But how did one buy a raincoat or umbrella while hitchhiking broke? "I'll take care of Miss Emers," Gus continued. "It *is* Miss?"

She nodded reluctantly. She might have insisted on Ms, but would not lie about Mrs—and doubted that it would have made any difference to this pair.

"So you get this crate going before it stalls out," Gus finished.

The driver should have bridled at the tone, but Thatch only shrugged and eased the motor into gear. The beat of rain on the windshield intensified as the vehicle picked up speed.

Gus put his big familiar hand on Zena's elbow. "There's clothing in back. Maybe some'll fit you. Don't worry about the rug; it'll dry."

"Thank you, no," she said, shaking him off. Already it was beginning! "Where's the next stop?"

9

"No next stop," he said. "You're staying with us. Now come on back." And once more that hand landed, this time on her wet shoulder.

She rammed a stiffened knuckle into his armpit and followed it up with a wrist grip that sent him twisting to the floor. "Thatch!" he cried as he went down, crashing against the dinette table so that it clattered to the floor. He sounded like a lost child.

Thatch brought the bus to a skidding halt that made Zena grab for the little sink. There was an entire kitchenette along this wall, including a range and a refrigerator, but she did not have the opportunity to appreciate it. She wanted to get out—but now she was several feet down from the only door, with Gus sprawled across the narrow hall between her and it.

Thatch whirled his padded basket seat around and threw off his seat belt. He stood on the elevation between the front chairs—a rise in the floor that perhaps made room for the motor below—and in his hand was a small pistol. "Do not move," he said.

From bad to worse! She was normally a keen judge of suspicious characters, but Thatch had fooled her.

Zena moved. Her foot jerked up and her shoe flew off, striking his knee. Her aim would have been better if it had not been for the restriction of her soaking clothing.

As his eyes followed that direction, she hurdled Gus and dived for the gun hand. It was not as great a distance as it seemed, for the motor home was compactly organized.

"Thatch!" Gus repeated. "I'm hurt!"

She got the gun hand and clubbed Thatch's wrist with the stiffened side of her own hand. Not hard enough; she lacked the training to be really effective. He did not let go. Instead his other arm came around to grab her. They wrestled clumsily, jammed between the two front seats, their feet skidding on the carpeted platform. But she got her shoulder into his chest and bent the gun hand back until his grip loosened.

10

Still Thatch clung to her with desperate strength, hugging her in a manner that would have been ludicrous if intended to be romantic and suicidal if combative—except for the gun. Obviously he knew nothing about fighting, and he was trying to restrain her rather than hurt her. At another time she might have appreciated the consideration, if that were what it was. Maybe they just didn't like damaged merchandise.

She wrestled the gun from his weakened grasp and swung it at his head. But his clumsy hold entangled her, and the blow only grazed his ear. The butt of the gun bent the earpiece of his glasses, and the lenses fell sidewise across his face, suspended from his other ear. The blow hurt, she was sure, but he did not collapse the way Gus had.

She hit him again, more squarely, but the gun lacked heft, and still he would not yield, though his glasses continued to dangle perilously against his chin. His hand wrenched at the back of her blouse, pulling it out of the band of the skirt, and they both tripped over Gus's legs and toppled. She did not have proper hold of the gun, and it fell out of her hand as she struggled to disengage herself from the two men.

"Thatch!" Gus cried again, though he was now only peripherally involved.

She caught Thatch's hand a second time and applied a finger grip, a submission hold. He was obviously the one she had to subdue; Gus was not even trying to help his friend.

"Now I want off this bus!" she gasped.

Thatch was adamant. "No."

"I can break your finger."

Still the fool would not give way. "You don't understand."

She put pressure on his hand and saw him whiten behind the tenuously hanging glasses. "Yes. Off!"

He shook his head, and finally the glasses fell. "No!"

11

She realized suddenly, and by no obscure intuition, that she could break his finger—and still it would not change his mind. He was impervious to compulsion. Yet obviously it was not sex that drove him; even in confused combat she could tell the difference between self defense and lascivious attack. He would have been more effective had he been less scrupulous about where he touched her. But he was one of those odd types who would not submit to pain. A masochist, possibly. He would keep coming after her, coming after her, as long as he was able.

"Gus only meant to help," Thatch gasped. "We can't let you go until you know the story—for your own good."

She was twisting his finger off, yet instead of screaming the agony she knew he felt he was trying to reason with her! "I know enough of the story," she said. "Two men pick up one girl—"

"To save you from the flood!" Gus cried, sitting up. She couldn't hold them both off much longer, if Gus became active. In a moment she would have to make another break for it. First, the gun—

Her actions under stress often preceded her thoughts. She let go of Thatch and snatched up the weapon. Both men regained their feet and stood looking at her. They were disheveled and wet in patches from the struggle, but seemed more concerned than afraid.

"Maybe we'd better let her off," Thatch said. He had recovered his glasses, the lenses miraculously unbroken.

"No 'let' about it!" Zena snapped. "When you try to gang up on a girl, and use a gun—"

"Look at the gun," Thatch said with a wry expression.

She looked, alert for a trick. She was no expert in handguns, though she was sure she could shoot straight if she had to. Most women were womanishly foolish about such things; not her. But this, she saw now, was not actually a pistol. It was an imitation, a mockup for a child. A realistic toy.

"I just wanted to keep you quiet long enough to talk to you," Thatch said.

Her glance flicked to the side. She could open the door and leap out before they could stop her, though she might have to clip someone again in the process. But what would she do out there in the pelting rain? Few cars were moving now, and fewer would be inclined to stop; and in just a few hours it would be too late anyway. Was escape really her best choice?

Obviously she had misjudged these men, to a degree. A toy gun! "I'm listening."

"It's going to rain a long time, Gus says. Maybe flooding, bad flooding. We have to stick to the highlands, the ridge, until we can get north out of the state and into the mountains. We're picking up people along the way."

"So I noticed." She set down the mock gun. "Why haven't you picked up men?"

Gus and Thatch exchanged glances. "It gets complicated," Thatch said. "Anyway, we meant you no harm, and if you really don't want to stay here, you can get off now. Gus just thought naturally you'd stay, and want to get dry."

She glanced across the dinette cubicle and out of the window. The rain was still coming down heavily, at the rate of about an inch an hour. She knew it *would* continue, and that there would indeed be severe flooding. The men, whatever their motive, had stumbled on the right idea—and their vehicle was ideal for it. If she had misjudged them—and it seemed increasingly likely that she had, at least to some extent—she could do worse than travel with them. Much worse. For now.

"I do want to get dry," she said. "But I don't want to be pawed."

Gus started to protest, but Thatch cut him off. "There's clothing and a bath in back. You can find them yourself. We'll be up front, driving."

Was she making a mistake? This seemed to represent

her best present hope for survival, even if it remained a minority chance. She nodded.

They squeezed aside, and Zena went back. She was still on guard against a fast move, but it didn't come. And why should it? If they wanted something special from her, they could always try for it later. So long as she stayed aboard.

She wasn't sure, now, that they did want anything special. They were a cozy twosome, with odd interdependencies.

The men took their seats in the driving section, and in a moment the vehicle started moving.

Zena found the clothing. The entire rear of the motor home was made into a beautiful couch that could convert into a full-size double bed large enough for three. Fair-sized windows were discreetly curtained for privacy. She wished she could lie down right then and sleep, forgetting all cares! Closets were on either side of the hall adjacent to this sitting-room/bedroom. One contained male attire, the other female.

Yet there was no other female aboard.

There were dresses, designed for a woman several inches taller and about forty pounds heavier than her. And they were a few decades out of style.

On the other hand, the male closet contained jeans and shirts to fit a high school boy. Obviously this motor home did not belong to the present occupants. Had they stolen it?

Zena closed the folding door across the hall and wedged into the boy's apparel. Tight, very tight across the hips, but it did feel better to be dry.

She moved up to the tiny bathroom cubicle next to the male closet, carrying her wadded clothing. There was a sink, toilet and shower economically fitted in. She wrung her clothing out in the first, used the second, and passed up the last: she had no need of another drenching.

She found a towel and worked her hair over quickly. It converted magically from a dark brown straggle to a light

14

brown dust mop. "Just call me Afro," she murmured, smiling into the little mirror. Not an attractive arrangement, for her; her features were too sharp, so that she fancied she looked like a witch. Her green eyes contributed to the effect. But it would do just fine until she learned more about her hosts.

She emerged, but stepped back to pause before the rear side window. The water beat against it stridently, blurring everything beyond. There was only a vague sense of motion, aside from the swaying of the vehicle itself. She might as well be looking into a murky aquarium, seeing the slow turbulence of some great fish. Was it safe to be driving now? Of course not—but it would be disaster *not* to drive!

She would have to watch it, with the men, whatever their motive. Twenty-five and single—she would not stay young forever. Of course, men were not all alike; they only seemed that way. Maybe she had overreacted to Gus's helping hand. Some people liked casual physical contact. But at least they knew, now, that she was not that type.

She felt a twinge of guilt. She could have been married three times over by now, had she *been* that type. She could not point to any traumatic betrayals to explain her attitude. She could not claim that it was merely a matter of failing to meet the right man; by any rational definition the men she had known had been right. Perhaps she merely preferred her independence, needing no one. But that answer didn't satisfy her any more than the other answers.

Life, in certain respects, was doubtless easier for women who could give and receive freely, however unwisely.

She took a short breath and blew it out. Threatening her with a toy pistol! Worse, she had fallen for it.

Still, it inevitably came back to this: who else was going her way? She couldn't tell anyone the significance of the rain, and she didn't have a car of her own. She was out of money; strangers wouldn't cash checks, and she had exhausted her small change on coffee that morning. Hitchhiking had been bad enough before the rain started—but she had feared the government would be watching the mass-transportation facilities. In a few days the government's attitude would be irrelevant, but if she were caught and detained today or tomorrow, it would be the end.

Thatch was still driving, with Gus peering ahead. The wide view provided by the windshield only made the weather seem worse. The rain pelted down in splendid savagery, making the deepening puddles dance. The fields beside the highway appeared already to be flooding, but the road itself was clear. Fortunately the interstate systems had good drainage. Visibility was so bad that Thatch was simply following the dotted line dividing two of the lanes, detouring around the increasingly frequent hulks of stalled cars.

Stalled cars. They seemed empty. What had happened to the people in them? Did they just disappear into the ground like ants from a disturbed nest? They would never return. . . .

There were no houses in sight. The rain made it seem as if they had driven into some primeval wilderness. Indeed, there was already some debris on it, the highway—flotsam from the scrub. The wild state was wasting no time encroaching. Fortunately the bus was tight and warm; seemingly not a drop of water had leaked inside. She could not, actually, have asked for a better ride.

"I'm sorry, boys," she said, taking her seat in the dinette just behind the driver's seat. "I was tired and hungry and wet and jumpy. I guess I got the wrong idea."

Gus turned, smiling. His seat was double-width, but mounted so that it could face around behind. He had an attractive grin and looked capable. But she could not forget that forlorn cry of his—"*Thatch!*"—as he was hurt. Not badly hurt, either! Was he in fact a physical coward, or was there something else between these two men?

16

"That's all right," Gus said. "Girl's got to watch out for herself. Where're you from?"

She took a moment to restore the dinette table, still fallen. It propped on a single light metal rod, now bent but not broken. Like Thatch's glasses.

Where was she from? What was the safest answer? She felt she owed no further allegiance to the government, but she was not yet ready to set aside her commitment to secrecy.

A half-truth would have to do. "The Cape. I worked there—for a while. How about you?"

"Other side of the street," Gus said, gesturing expansively. "State, I mean." He seemed to carry no grudge. "Too hot for regular work, not much money, so Thatch got us this bus to drive north. The owner pays for gas and tolls, and we have a week to get it safely to Michigan."

Zena shook her head silently. It was nice to know they had come by the vehicle honestly—but it would never see Michigan, now that the rain had started.

"Just in time, too," Gus continued. "I figured the rain was coming, and I knew we had to get moving fast. We just stopped off for cheap gas—can't get that on the main route—and then we saw you."

Fine. Keep the men talking about themselves. "You had trouble finding decent work? Maybe you should have gone back to school to learn a trade."

"I've been to school," Gus said amiably. "You wouldn't know it to look at me, but I've got a BA in Liberal Arts."

Zena smiled carefully. Liberal arts, by one definition, was the way a dull student could get through college without having to learn anything. "You're right. I wouldn't know it."

"Say—are you a karate instructor or something?"

Fair question, after the fighting she had just done. "No. If I had been an instructor, Thatch would never have gotten a hand on me. I'm a meteorologist. I happened to take a course in self-defense. Just in case."

17

"Meteorology!" he exclaimed. She thought he was going to make the old joke about studying meteors, but he passed that up. "Then you know about this rain!"

Trouble again! "What do you mean?"

"That's what you do, isn't it? Study the weather? So you know."

"I study the weather, yes. But that doesn't necessarily mean I know more than you do about this particular rain. Obviously I didn't know enough to come in out of it!"

Gus let out a hearty laugh. Then he shook his head wisely. "Uh-*uh!* This is a *special* rain! It started with that band in the sky—you saw that, didn't you?"

"No." Literally true. But the man was on an uncomfortably accurate track—by what coincidence, she hoped to learn.

"This one that looked like a contrail, then got larger and larger until it filled the whole sky? They said it was just a freak cloud formation that would go away in a few days, but the experts always lie about things like that. How could you miss it?"

"I wasn't there."

"Zena, the whole world could see it! The news was censored out of the papers, which is how I knew it was significant, but I have a little shortwave radio and I picked up the hams discussing it. That band went all around the earth from pole to pole, like a Russian satellite. But the Russians didn't know anything about it either. Not the ones who were talking, anyway. You would have had to be blind or in jail to miss it!"

No help for it: She was not a facile evader, and she refused to lie directly. "I wasn't *on* the world."

Gus chuckled. "Oh, yeah! You came from the Cape. You were up in orbit, right?"

"That's right."

"So you didn't see it after all. Not from below, anyhow! Maybe you were investigating it from a satellite?"

"No. Let's talk about something else."

"I get it now. Military secret."

"Something like that." Did it really make any difference? The damage had been done before Gus ever spotted his band in the sky, and there was no way to reverse it now.

"Well, the way I see it, this is no ordinary rain," Gus said. "It's a canopy-rain, coming down from the Saturn-rings."

"Saturn is another planet!" Zena exclaimed, relieved to discover that he was after all off the track. It had seemed for a moment that he had somehow guessed the truth. The truth that she was still theoretically not permitted to divulge.

"I said Saturn-*rings*. Rings of ice, like those around Saturn—only they're around Earth now. So the rain won't stop—not for a long, long time. Maybe the whole world will flood. Right?"

Now she was intrigued. He was veering closer to the track again. "What are you talking about?"

"You know. You're the meteorologist. I only know what I read."

"That's right. I'm the meteorologist—and I can't make much sense of what you're saying. What's this about a canopy, or rings of ice?"

"That theory. How there were rings of ice around the world, long ago. And they melted down into a canopy, and then into rain—so much that the oceans rose up maybe a mile, and never did go down again. That's what the Bible is really talking about, and all those other legends of the flood. And it's starting again!"

"I never heard of such a thing!" Zena said indignantly. "There's no fossil record of such large increases in the ocean level—not in the past billion years, certainly!"

"Oh yes there *is*," he insisted. "Just in the last million years the ocean has changed—"

"Fluctuated, yes; risen, no," she said. "You're thinking of the last ice age, when so much water was taken up by glaciers and polar ice that the level of the world's oceans dropped—then rose again when all that ice melted. But that has nothing to do with any canopy—"

"Yes it *does*! And ancient man actually *saw* the canopy."

"Ridiculous! What ancient man saw were the four great glacials of the Pleistocene: Gunz, Mindel, Riss and Wurm."

"The four frost giants," Gus agreed. "But it was the *canopy* that caused those glaciers. Say—didn't they have American names, too?"

"There were equivalent glacials in North America. The Nebraskan, Kansan, Illinoisian and Wisconsin. They were named after the states in which the first finds were made—the moraines and scratches and other typical signs. The European ones were named after the various German valleys where they were identified. The two sets correlate pretty well."

"Right! So there was one overall cause, worldwide. The canopy."

"Gus, if man had seen anything like that, he would have recorded it somehow, if only in legends."

"He *did*. Ancient pottery shows the canopy, and Stonehenge was built to—"

She laughed. "I don't know what sort of stuff you read, but that's crackpot theory! Are you sure it wasn't a fantasy novel?"

"Nonfiction," he said seriously. "It was the Annular Theory. I have a book on it packed away, *Heavens and Earth of Prehistoric Man.* Things like that interest me. I'll show you, when we have a chance to unload."

"So that's why you think this rain will flood the world!" she said derisively. "You read someone's wild conjecture—"

But Gus was not nettled. Whatever his failings, he had a steady temper. "Do you know otherwise?"

That shut her up. She did not know otherwise. In fact

20

this theory of his bore an uncanny resemblance to the actual situation. It was as if fate had directed her to the very person who could understand and help—a person she would never ordinarily have met. She knew the rain *would* continue, horrendously, even though she was not free to admit that. Everything she had learned in space was classified, rightly or wrongly. Her flight from the stupidity and confusion that had precipitated this crisis did not release her from the oath of secrecy she had unwillingly taken.

But if Gus came close to the truth, was she bound to lie in defense of that secrecy? Or was it ethical to let him prevail, so long as she never specifically confirmed his accuracy?

"So we figure the whole state will flood out, maybe in a few days, and we're headed for the mountains," Gus said, satisfied. "We've got the Whole Earth catalogue and extra gasoline, a fifty-gallon reserve tank we won't touch until we have to. And food."

"Food?" she said eagerly.

"Hey yeah, you're hungry! Here." Gus got up and stepped past her to the kitchenette. He got a loaf of bread and opened the refrigerator. "Mostly jars of stuff—we figured it would keep better, because we won't always have current for the fridge. And we didn't have too much money. Bean or marmalade?"

"What?"

"Your sandwich. We have other stuff, but it isn't open yet. Don't want to waste anything."

"Oh." She got up, feeling her fatigue now that she had had a chance to rest. "I'll do it."

Gus shrugged and turned over the makings. She made herself one of each.

"So it's like this," Gus said as she munched sandwiches that hunger made delicious and washed them down with a glass of milk. "Maybe the whole nation will flood out, with only a few islands where the mountain tops are. No one will be left, except us. We don't have an ark, so we'll

21

have to use this bus. And we'll save civilization. Like Noah."

Zena had to laugh, explosively. Fatigue and relief had abated her inhibitions. Precious crumbs of bean sandwich sprayed out of her mouth in most unladylike fashion, embarrassing her. "Noah!"

But Gus was serious. "That's why we're picking up people. We don't need old ones or sick ones—but every young, healthy person is a potential citizen of the new order."

Suddenly it wasn't funny—if it had ever been. She had been preoccupied by the problems of the moment, and hadn't thought it through: people were going to die. Including her own family, if she didn't get through in time to warn them. Had she herself been picked up because she was a woman of childbearing age?

"Make sense to you?" Gus asked, averting his gaze.

It made sense, all right! These two hoped to build a captive kingdom! Would she have been accepted as a candidate if she had not been pretty? Ha-ha! "I believe I'll get off at the next mountain," she said.

Gus made a gesture of laissez-faire. "It has to be voluntary, of course. But you'll drown, here."

The awful thing was that it was true. She *would* drown, if she didn't get out of Florida in the next few days. And as the nature of the disaster became apparent to the surviving populace, a woman alone would not be safe. From either the weather or the people.

"If you really believe that the world in this vicinity is coming to an end," she said, "why aren't you worried about your own folks? You *do* have folks?"

Gus wasn't fazed. "My dad farms in the mountains. My brother was captain of his school swimming team. They can take care of themselves."

"And yours?" she asked Thatch.

Thatch didn't answer.

"He knows we can't save anyone else until we save our-

22

selves," Gus said. "If there's a break in the rain, then maybe we can look about."

"A pragmatic philosophy," she said. "It confirms my opinion of you. How about dropping me off when you hit the Appalachians, then?"

If Gus caught the irony he didn't show it. "Sure enough. But you're eating our food and using up our gas. You'll have to earn your keep."

She tensed. "Such as?"

"Such as cleaning house, washing socks, sewing buttons—"

"I'm a meteorologist! I never sewed a button in my life!"

"Well, there's a sewing machine in back. *We* don't know how to use it."

"Neither do I!" she snapped.

Gus looked at her with annoying tolerance. "Being feminine bugs you, doesn't it."

Perfect shot! Her first impulse was to hit him again, to make him go down with another wail for his buddy. Her second was to launch a tirade on masculine arrogance. But she was better rested now, and dry, and not so hungry, and her more sober third impulse prevailed. She would not be baited! "All right—I'll sew buttons!"

Gus shrugged with just one shoulder, knowing he had the upper hand now. "You don't have to. That was only an example."

"Yes I do have to," she said with controlled fury. "Because I have other values, and I'm not joining your kingdom."

The vehicle slowed. "There's one," Thatch said.

Another pickup. "Male or female?" Zena asked.

"Female," Gus said, swinging around to look. "Young. And single. We don't even stop for nonsurvival types. I told you."

"Do you mean you leave them standing, knowing they

will drown?" she demanded. But that required no answer: of course they did.

It was female, all right. A tall girl with long blonde hair, her breasts standing out like turrets in the plastered mess that was her dress. Zena was relieved to see her; a statuesque blonde was exactly what was needed to distract the men.

Gus got out of his seat and pushed open the door as the motor-home halted. The sound of the rain became loud, making Zena shiver. "Welcome aboard!" Gus cried, extending his big hand.

"Thank you, sir," the blonde answered. Her voice was low and husky, as befitted her appearance. A sex bomb, despite what originally had been reasonably decorous apparel. She stepped up lithely, showing muscular legs above the tall heels. She was shorter than Gus, but not by much. "That rain! Will it never stop?"

"It never will!" Gus said cheerfully. "Get it moving, Thatch."

Thus did another fly walk into the spider's nest. Wait until Blondie heard about the onerous duties of citizenship!

"What's your name?" Gus asked. "I'm Gus; this is Thatch, and she's Zena."

"Gloria," she said, smiling properly. "Gloria Black. My car ran out of gas, and no one would stop! I'm soaked!"

"Horrors!" Zena muttered behind her hand.

"There's dry clothing in back," Gus said, putting his familiar hand on her damp shoulder. Zena winced. "I'll show you."

"Thank you," Gloria said, ultimately feminine even when dripping. She did not seem to find it remarkable to be welcomed in to a traveling bedroom. Zena resented the type but found it expedient to remain silent.

"Do you know how to sew?" Gus inquired.

"Excellently."

"Well, let me tell you where we're going," Gus said enthusiastically. "You know, there's a sewing machine here! This rain won't stop. We have food—"

"That's fine, but I'm only going to Gainesville."

"I'd better explain," Gus said, guiding her back. "This rain—"

Zena transferred to the seat Gus had vacated, so that she could talk to Thatch privately. The chair was capacious and comfortable; one could readily fall asleep in it. But what a contrast to the fury of nature outside, so thoroughly visible here! "Hello," she said.

Thatch's eyes flicked over to her, then back to the road. He didn't answer. The rain made driving dangerous, even at the moderate speed he was going, but he could talk if he wanted to. She wondered if the heat of physical struggle had made him forget his shyness before, while her direct approach in the absence of Gus choked him up.

"I'm sorry I hit you," she said.

"Forget it." She could see his knuckles whiten on the wheel. Gus might readily forgive; but not this man.

"If I hurt you, I'll try to clean it up," she said. "I *am* sorry, Thatch. I thought you had a real gun, and I overreacted." How much easier it was to apologize to an unhandsome man, as though he were less dangerous!

"It's not that," he said tightly.

"You aren't much for socializing, are you?" It was amazing how his obvious discomfort made her feel at ease; not long ago Gus had teased her similarly.

He smiled momentarily, still not looking at her. In that moment his weak-chinned, scarred face gained strength. "Gus takes care of that sort of thing."

She was tempted to inquire exactly what the relation between the two men was, but refrained. Some men preferred men, particularly those brought up in fatherless households. If this were his case, it really was not her business. In fact, that would verify that she had been mistaken about Gus's familiarity; it could be his camouflage for a basic disinterest in the opposite sex.

Well, blonde Gloria would soon be the proof of that pudding! In any event, it behooved Zena to comprehend the real motives of Gus and Thatch. She might well be eating and working with them for several days in close quarters. "Do you do all the driving?"

"Gus doesn't have a license." She was surprised; she had anticipated a demurral. "Was it revoked?"

"No, he never learned to drive." Thatch was speaking more freely, now that they were talking about another person. He was shy and basically harmless; even when goaded to action by a threat to his friend, he had used that toy pistol!

"Well, *I* have a license," she said. How much better to drive, even through this weather, than to sew buttons!

"You're not part of the party."

If Gus had said that, it would have had another meaning. "So you go along with everything Gus says?"

Thatch nodded affirmatively.

"If you trust me to fix your food," she said, "you should trust me to drive."

"It's not that, Miss Emers. Gus has firm notions of propriety. Women don't drive."

"Call me Zena," she said, knowing he wouldn't.

Sure enough, he didn't answer. His arms tightened again, and he stared straight ahead.

"You can't do all the driving!" she exclaimed. "In this weather it must be an awful strain."

"The job must be done."

There wasn't much to say to that, so she just watched ahead. There had been other traffic at the start of the rain, for the interstate was a busy highway. Now the moving traffic had thinned. It had been raining for an hour; many cars had stalled. Thatch went around them, maneuvering with skill.

Most of the traffic must have gotten under cover as the deluge had intensified. A number of vehicles were evidently waiting it out; they were pulled to the sides, dark lumps beyond the spray.

Zena shook her head. In time the water would rise up about them, and it would be too late for the hapless occupants. She wanted to cry the alarm—but even if she were not bound by paramilitary restrictions, it would be a hopeless task. There were hundreds, probably thousands of cars waiting; she could not warn them all. And if she could the people would not believe her. Why play Cassandra, the prophetess of doom?

Gloria and Gus returned. The blonde *did* know how to sew, and rapidly, too: she was wearing one of the outsize dresses Zena had passed over, and now it fit her spectacularly.

"So you don't believe the rain will stop," Gloria commented as they sat down in the dinette. She peered forward worriedly. "I do hope you're mistaken."

"I'm not mistaken," Gus said. "Zena here's a meteorologist. She was up in orbit watching the whole thing. She'll tell you."

"I have said nothing about it." Zena protested.

"You don't have to. You know I'm right—that's why you're coming along, even though you don't like men."

"I didn't say that, either," Zena said. If she had had something in her hand she would have thrown it at him, hard.

Gloria's eyes narrowed speculatively. "Could I talk to you a moment, dear, privately?" she asked Zena.

And what did she have in *her* bleach-headed mind, Zena wondered. This group was not shaping up to her liking! But she nodded, reining her temper. "If you wish."

They went to the bedroom/lounge and pulled the door across. "*Are* you a meteorologist?" Gloria asked, her voice low so that it could not be overheard.

Zena had expected a question on a different topic, but this was just as bad.

"He's serious," the other woman said. "He believes the

27

entire state is going to flood—and you aren't denying it. I'm not one to place credence in a wild notion like that, but—"

Zena shrugged.

"I saw that band in the sky," Gloria said. "It alarmed me. But I have a special reason to be concerned, so I hope you will tell me the truth."

Zena would have been angry at this affront to her integrity, but realized that in this circumstance it was a fair question. "Either the rain will stop—or it won't. I can't help you."

"Be patient, dear. This is difficult, and I may have to get off soon anyway. Gus wants me to—"

"To help restore civilization after the flood has wiped out the rest of humanity," Zena finished. "He thinks we're part of his post-deluge empire."

Gloria looked at her, one brow arched. "I suppose that's one way of putting it. So if the rain is that bad—and at this stage I'm almost ready to accept that!—it will be awkward."

"I have already tried to make that plain to them. They think I'm merely being difficult."

Gloria began to color. "More than awkward. You see, I am not quite what I appear to be. Ordinarily it doesn't matter, but if it really floods—"

"Suddenly I don't follow you."

"I am not a woman. Not physically."

Zena cocked her head. "Would you spell that out in monosyllables, please—dear?"

"I have a male body."

Now Zena stared. "You say you are a *man*?"

"A transvestite, if you will, though that isn't quite accurate. Male body in female clothing."

"I don't believe it!"

"The matter is subject to verification, if you insist."

Zena realized with a growing shock that she meant it. "No—I'll take your word!"

Gloria looked relieved. "Thank you. So you see, I would not be much help in what Mr. Gunter has in mind. I wish it were otherwise."

Zena rather suspected that it *was* otherwise, but she wasn't going to gamble. "Why—"

"Why do I dress like a woman? That would be tedious to explain at the moment. Right now I have to know: is it really going to flood—the way they think?"

Zena sighed. "Yes, it really will."

"So that there may be hundreds of feet of water?"

"There may be."

"Then I suppose I'd better explain things to the others. I cannot remain with this group under false pretenses."

Zena studied her/him carefully. There was no sign that this was not a woman. Could this be some elaborate defense mechanism? Still, she remembered those muscular legs as Gloria had first stepped up into the vehicle. Those would be normal, for a man. She stifled what threatened to become a hysterical laugh. "No, I think you should surprise them with it one romantic evening."

Gloria smiled—and did the maleness show in that expression now? "I have surprised men most unpleasantly upon occasion," she said.

Now a peep got loose. Zena covered her mouth. "I can imagine!" Actually she did not find it funny so much as acutely embarrassing. But what was the proper reaction to a confidence like this? Either an extremely mixed-up woman stood before her—or a man.

"For a short trip, no confession would be necessary or desirable," Gloria said. "But in a case like this, with close proximity for many days—"

Zena finally sobered. "I understand." God, what complications!

They went forward. "Got it all worked out, girls?" Gus demanding, smiling.

"Not exactly," Gloria said. "About this business of picking up girls—"

29

"We're picking up young, healthy people," Gus said quickly. Zena noted his defensive reaction. What was he hiding?

Gloria shook his head. "I would like to join your party. But there is something I have to tell you."

"It's voluntary, of course," Gus said quickly, becoming accommodating as he saw the plum dropping into his hand. Zena bit her tongue to suppress a nervous giggle.

"I'm afraid you don't understand," Gloria said, blushing again. Zena had another moment of doubt: if Gloria were not female, a terrific amount of practice must have gone into that blush! Zena herself very seldom colored.

"Oh-oh," Gus said. "You married?"

"No, not married! But I'm not—"

"Not another wallflower!" Gus groaned. "Zena here doesn't much like men, either."

"Don't blame Zena," Gloria said. "The truth is—"

Thatch slowed the vehicle. "Flooded ahead," he announced.

"Splash on through it," Gus said irritably, not appreciating the distraction.

"The motor may quit."

"Then start it again!" Gus returned to Gloria. "Now look, you can't be squeamish about—"

"You can't start a wet motor," Thatch said.

"Then dry it off!" Gus yelled. He had, it seemed, an answer for everything—except what Zena knew was coming. Served him right! "Girls, I don't know what you're getting at."

Meanwhile the flood was close at hand. Obedient to Gus's directive, Thatch maintained speed and drove into it. The water sprayed high on either side and the bus slowed. Zena heard the wash of liquid against the underside, and it made her nervous. The motor *would* quit—and there would be no drying it, in this continual rain. Yet delay was intolerable!

30

Then the vehicle rose out of it and rolled over solid asphalt again. "See?" Gus said smugly.

But they were entering a lowlands section of the highway, and there was more flooding ahead. Gloria did not have opportunity to make his statement before they were splashing again.

The second area was deeper—eighteen inches at least. And in the center of it, the motor stalled.

# Chapter 2: Flood

Zena felt as though a judge had just passed a sentence of life imprisonment on her. Stuck without power, perhaps two hundred miles from the security of the mountains.

"Start it! Start it!" Gus cried. There was a kind of whine in his voice, reminiscent of his cry for help when hurt.

Thatch tried, turning the ignition switch to the starter again and again, but the motor was dead. Now the beat of rain on the roof seemed louder.

"Let it alone," Zena said wearily as the battery began to fade. "If we run the current down, we'll *never* get it going!"

"We shall have to push it," Gloria said.

"No!" Gus cried. Now the overtone of desperation was unmistakable. How quickly his confidence degenerated during stress! "The water's up to the floorboards!"

"Maybe we should leave it here and walk," Zena said without enthusiasm. One thing she knew: they had to keep moving, or they were all dead.

"No!" Gus screamed. "Start the motor!"

Gloria looked at him with an expression Zena understood, for she felt the same. What was wrong with handsome Gus, that he shied away from anything difficult or messy?

"I hate to get wet again," Gloria said. "But if you're right about the flooding, we can't afford to stay here. One of us will have to steer; the others can get out and—"

"No!" Gus cried again. "Not the girls!"

"We are not made of sugar and spice," Zena said. "I'll push."

"But first," Gloria said firmly, "I have to tell you—"

Zena had to interrupt. "I don't think this is the time, after all." If there were to be a scene, it should be scheduled when all hands weren't needed for an emergency.

Gloria ignored her. She/he removed his long blonde hair.

Gus and Thatch both stared. Under that fair wig was a dark crew cut.

"She shaved her head!" Gus exclaimed, not catching on.

Gloria opened his blouse and reached inside, around behind his back. In a moment his full bra was unhooked. It came away solidly, leaving a bare masculine chest.

Now Gus comprehended—or thought he did. "A fairy!" he exclaimed.

Gloria turned to him. "Say that again, and I will flatten your nose against your lying face. I am a transvestite, not a homosexual—and I have in the past done police work."

"Thatch!" Gus cried, falling back.

Police work, Zena thought. Policemen dressed like women, walking through parks at night so as to lure unsuspecting thieves and rapists! But why should such an undercover agent be illegally hitchhiking on the interstate?

Thatch stepped between Gus and Gloria, smaller than

33

either but abruptly possessed of initiative. "What's the idea, pretending to be a woman?"

"It is not something you would readily understand," the man said with a dignity marred only by his lipsticked lips and pendant earrings. "I do not like exposing my identity to you in this fashion. But there is work to be done. Stand aside."

Thatch considered, then yielded to the tone of authority and gave way. The transvestite stepped out of the dress and stood only in lacy feminine panties—but there could now be no question about his physical masculinity. His lacquered fingernails and toenails were incongruous.

"Call me Gordon," he said, and opened the door. Again the rain blasted in, a terror in its ferocity. "I will push— alone if need be. We'll talk later."

The water was indeed up to the floorboards. The bottom step was below the surface of the tormented lake that extended as far as they could see. There was something fascinating about the way the neat shag rug extended up to the edge—of troubled water.

Gordon stepped down, almost knee-deep in the pool. Zena followed him, plunging in before she could change her mind. The sluice from the sky struck her head and shoulders as though determined to scour the features from her face, and the shock of chill water jumped up above her knees. She shivered and proceeded.

A gust of wind caught at her, almost sweeping her into a full immersion. She stumbled, but Gordon's hand was at her elbow, holding her erect with surprising strength. Now that he was almost naked, she wondered how she ever could have mistaken him for a woman.

"That took guts," she said.

He did not pretend to misunderstand. "I want to join this group, at least until this storm abates," he said. "But not under false pretenses. And Gloria doesn't like to get wet."

"You talk as if Gloria is a different person!"

34

"I'm the different person," he said.

"You're not going to arrest anybody?" She was trying to be facetious, but it didn't sound right.

"I did police work, but I really wasn't a policeman. It was more like a stake-out. Thought I might make myself useful. But it wasn't my style. I just prefer—being myself."

Being Gloria, he meant. To him, the male identity was no more than a necessary evil, a temporary state for emergencies like massive flooding. Well, she thought, it was his life.

They trod back toward the rear of the vehicle. One more figure descended from the open door: Thatch.

"We'll have to time our push together," Thatch shouted over the beat of the rain. "This bus is heavy, and the water will drag."

So it was happening again, Zena thought through her misery of renewed drenching. Thatch was an unimpressive, somewhat shy man—but when a challenge came, his competence expanded. Gus was the opposite.

The three lined up along the back, partly sheltered from the downpour, and shoved. At first it seemed the vehicle would not budge—but that was because the water made progress difficult to ascertain. From here to the graying fringe of visibility, there was no reference point except the oblong bulk of the motor-home. It *was* moving, slowly, for their feet gradually fell behind. And it was deepening; the water climbed slowly to her waist.

Was this the future of the world? A lake of troubled water with no shore? The overall rise of the oceanic level should not be more than two thousand feet—just about enough to submerge the eastern half of the continent. Anyone who made it to a suitable elevation would be all right.

Pushing the vehicle was tedious, fatiguing work. Zena was gasping after a minute, and the men were not much better off. How much did this box weigh? Six tons? What would they do when it came to an uphill push?

"Rest!" Thatch cried, and they stopped. The rain was still cold, but now it was refreshing; such expenditures of energy were great for generating body heat.

"We don't have enough manpower," Gordon said. "We'll never make it this way."

Thatch nodded. They slogged on around to the driver's side. Zena actually found it easier to swim, because of the height of the water on her. "Can't do it," Thatch called in.

Gus rolled down the window a crack. "I didn't ask for excuses!" he yelled. "Just get this bus out of here!"

Zena was speechless at this arrogance. Gus, the biggest and probably the strongest among them, physically, relegated to steering duty though he could not drive. Gus, inside because he was afraid to get his feet wet—this man now took it upon himself to order them to do the impossible!

"The thing's too heavy," Thatch explained. Zena was annoyed to note the apologetic tone. "We can't push it uphill."

"Well, I won't let you in until you do!" Gus said, closing the window.

Thatch looked at the other two, and they looked at him. "Just got to get it up out of the water," Thatch said.

Now Zena exchanged a glance with Gordon. What were they to do? Break in and haul Gus out?

Thatch walked around to the back, paddling the water with his hands to speed the progress. There was a ladder there, leading up to an external luggage rack on the roof. He climbed up and peeked under the tarpaulin. "Two bikes and some rope!" he called down.

"Rope?" Zena repeated, seeing a possibility.

"If you're thinking of pulling it out," Gordon said, "remember that the weight's the same. We need leverage."

"Yes. A pulley," she agreed.

"Which we don't have."

Thatch climbed down. "We'll need tools—a wrench at least. There's one inside."

"We can't *get* inside," Zena pointed out.

"Ask Gus to throw it out."

Zena sloshed around to the front. At least, she mused, this immersion would stretch her tight jeans. Though probably not the way she wanted. "Gus—wrench!" she shouted.

The window lowered a crack. "What for?"

"I don't know. Thatch needs it."

"Promise?"

Zena stamped her foot in exasperation. Deep in water, with the rain attacking the rest of her, it was a wasted effort. "Yes! Do you think we're going to start breaking windows to get in? If we can't move it, we'll just have to wade on and leave you here."

He considered. Obviously those outside had the ultimate control of the situation. "All right." The window closed.

That might, she thought, actually be the best solution. Leave Gus and bus, go north afoot.

After about ninety seconds the window reopened. An object flew out, splashing into the water. "Thanks!" Zena called wryly to the closing window as she fished for the wrench. She had to hold her breath and dive down to do it. "I might even *find* it in a few minutes, if the current doesn't wash it away!"

The two men had the rope and bicycles down when she returned. "Screwdriver," Thatch said.

*Now* he told her! Wordlessly, Zena handed over the wrench and went back for the screwdriver.

They had the wheels off the bikes by the time she got back. Then they went to work on the tires, letting out the air and prying the rubber off the rims.

"A pulley!" Zena exclaimed, gazing at the first stripped wheel. "Someone has a brain! But will it work?"

Neither man answered, and she realized the question

had been pointless. It *had* to work, or the bus would be stranded in the rising flood.

"Survey the rope," Thatch told her brusquely. "How many feet?"

For a moment she was annoyed at being addressed as though she were a servant. But she realized that this was the other face of Thatch, the problem-solving side. Far better this than capitulation to the threat of the elements.

She climbed the little ladder and poked her head under the tarp. She became aware of the rain again, blasting volubly at the heavy canvas, and she shivered. How nice it would be to be inside the bus, dry and moving.

There were three hanks of sturdy nylon clothesline, thousand-pound test by the look of it. She had used similar for swings and around-the-house jobs after her father grew too ill to do them. Two were evidently fifty-foot lengths, the third a hundred feet. "Two hundred feet, in three pieces!" she called down.

"Three wheels, then," Thatch muttered. "Don't want to cut it unnecessarily."

Gordon tried the cord against the rim of one wheel. The rope was much smaller in diameter than the original tire, so the fit was quite loose; but the metal ridges held it in well.

"Survey for anchoring points," Thatch told Zena.

This was too much. "Don't order me about!" she snapped.

Thatch set the last wheel against the rear of the vehicle and started out himself, shading his eyes with his hand to peer through the mist.

"I'll do it!" Zena cried, chagrined. She had objected to female work; how could she object to male work now? "I'm sorry. Tell me what you want."

"We'll both do it," he said. "Visibility's too poor for one." If he were pleased at his victory, or even aware of it, he did not show it. He was merely doing his job, taking

38

each hazard as it came—including difficult females. Zena found herself at a loss to adjust to such an attitude; she was accustomed to push-and-shove, action and reaction.

They moved out, ploughing through water that seemed to be rising even as they searched. She tried to swim, but that was little better; there was a current in it. The water was tugging her somewhere, making her uneasy despite her other discomforts. Where was this lake going? What might be carried along in it? Old tires? Broken bottles? Dead horses?

They spotted the lined posts of a guard rail, well anchored but almost submerged. And a tall, firmly-positioned direction sign. Other than these, all was blank water. There were trees, but they were set far back from the highway, useless for this purpose.

"Three tie-ons should do it, for a start," Thatch said. "Fifty, one hundred, and one-fifty."

"I don't see how—" Zena started.

Thatch headed back, not trying to explain. Damn him!

Gordon had split the end of one length of line and formed it into two little loops. These he hooked over the projecting ends of one bicycle wheel's axle, and fastened them in place by screwing the wheel-nuts down tight against them. The arrangement made little sense to Zena. Obviously the wheel could now be hung from the rope in such a way that it would turn freely, but one turning wheel would hardly provide the leverage required.

"We have anchorages," Thatch said. "Fifty, one hundred, and one-fifty feet."

"Wrong ratios," Gordon said, completing the split-end mounting of another wheel. "Twenty-five, fifty and one hundred is the most we can do—a little less, actually, allowing for the ties and the wheel diameters. I hope the rope can take the strain, even so. Here, I'll show you."

Gordon produced a crayon and drew on the glass of the bus's back window. The lines were waxy and faint, but could be followed:

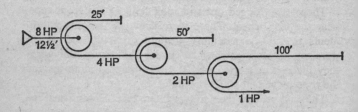

"You see, we have a three-stage reduction system," Gordon said. "Each pully doubles the force, reducing the forward motion by half. By the time it gets to the load—which will be the bus—our projected one horsepower of pull has become eight horsepower. But our hundred feet of forward motion has become only twelve and a half. No way around that; we've got to give up distance in favor of power. And we won't really get that much power; maybe fifty per cent will be taken up by the inefficiency of the system. Wheel resistance, rope friction, and so forth. But it should be enough to get the job done, eventually."

"But the rope's only good for a thousand pounds," Zena protested. "Half a ton. The bus must weigh ten times that!"

"Good point, and I *am* concerned," Gordon said. "But there are mitigations. The cord around each wheel is in effect doubled, and we can double the high-tension link too. That should give us a ton—and of course we're hauling, not lifting. If we're careful. . . ."

Yes, he had thought it out. What a change from sexy blonde Gloria! Gordon was a more practical male than he chose to let himself believe.

Tediously they set it up and strung it out. They made the anchorages to the posts of the fence, and fastened the base rope to the front of the motor home. "Take off the brakes!" Thatch yelled to Gus.

Then they trudged out and took hold of the front rope, near the lead wheel. There were some last-minute adjustments to get the assembly straight; actually the wheels were out of sight as they lay under the water. But when they made a concerted pull the bike wheels came up and the rope moved. It was working!

They moved the bus forward ten feet. Then Zena ran back to prop the wheels while the men held on. The resistance of the system that made the hauling hard also helped them hold it in place between pulls. Gus could have used the brakes, but it seemed better to leave him out of it for now.

Another set of attachments, another ten or twelve feet. And another, and another. Hours passed, and the gloom of evening closed in, and still the rain pelted down mercilessly. There seemed to be no one living in all the world except the three of them—and of course lazy Gus, dry and warm inside.

Zena felt the first stirrings of what she suspected could blossom into a full-fledged hate-affair. This preposterous situation!

At last they reached unflooded roadbed. And Gus let them in. But it was not the comfort she had expected in her delirium of fatigue. The motor had been dead for hours and the interior was chill.

"We've got to caulk this crate," Gus said. "The water came in. The rug's ruined!"

Zena stifled another hysterical laugh. "The rug!"

"Not only that," Gus continued seriously. "The refrigerator's stopped."

Cold as she was, Zena hardly cared. She moved back to poke into the closets, seeking more dry clothing. Even one of those dowdy dresses would do.

41

"Water must have snuffed the pilot light," Gordon said. "That's of small moment. But you're right: we can't let the water flood us out every time we pass through a lake. We'll have to seal off every access. We can put plastic sheeting over the external access panels, braced by hardboard and sealed over with furnace tape. Main problems will be the passenger door and the engine compartment. We'll have to forage for what we need."

Gus looked at him. "You know, I think I like you better as a man. You've got a head for practicalities."

Exactly Zena's thought. Gordon did not deign to answer.

Zena found a warm dress and shut herself into the bathroom to change. She could hear the men talking, despite the noise of rain outside.

"Now get the engine going!" Gus told Thatch.

"I don't know anything about motors!" Thatch protested.

"I do," Gordon interjected. "Gloria's a fool about cars—that's why we ran out of gas. But I can—"

"You can start it?" Gus cried happily.

"I'll need a light, and some shelter when I lift the exterior access panel. So the rain doesn't short it out all over again. And some dry cloth, and tools."

"Fix him up!" Gus snapped to Thatch.

"There's an interior access," Thatch said. By the sound of it, he was rummaging in the closets.

"Why so there is!" Gordon exclaimed. "Beautiful!"

Zena emerged from the bathroom to find Gordon at work between the two front seats. She didn't know what he did, but before long there was the blessed roar of the motor. They were on their way again!

She slept for an hour on the back couch, then woke as the bus stopped. For a moment she thought it meant more flooding, but then she heard a woman's sharp voice.

"Three men?" the unseen female inquired. "Long trip north? I'm hungry and I'm wet, but I'm not ripe for harem duty yet! Move on—I'll take my chances here!"

After more dialogue, too low to be intelligible, the door closed and they moved on. Zena smiled, thinking of the harem accusation. The nomenclature was wrong. A harem would be one man and three women. Then she frowned, realizing that the nameless woman would probably pay for her spirit with her life. Where would she find another lift to the mountains?

Harem ... she thought as she drifted back to sleep.

She dreamed of being decked out in filmy petticoat-trousers, waiting for the Sultan.

Abruptly she was awake. Harem! That was what Gus and Thatch had been planning! Obvious all along, but she had somehow blinded herself to it. Nothing so ambitious as an empire—just making time while the sun shone.

She peered out at the rain. Sun?

That faceless girl—left behind to die, just because she had pride and spunk.

Zena was on her feet. "Turn around!" she screamed, rushing up the passage.

Gus and Gordon, nodding in the dining alcove, snapped alert. "What?" Gus demanded.

"You left a girl out there to die," Zena accused him. "Now turn about and go back and pick her up!"

"Are you crazy? That was an hour ago!" Gus said.

"Twenty-five minutes ago," Gordon corrected him, looking at his dainty feminine watch.

"I don't care how long ago!" Zena yelled, sounding hysterical in her own ears. "Thatch, you turn around."

"Uh-*uh*," Gus said. "She didn't want to come."

"Because you threatened her with—*turn* it, Thatch!"

"She's got a point," Gordon said. "I haven't felt easy about that myself. At least we could have given her a lift to high ground."

"Look," Gus said reasonably. "We never threatened her

43

with anything. You're not even interested in women, are you? She jumped to a conclusion."

"Then we should have disabused her of that conclusion," Gordon said, the color rising to his face.

Gus raised his two hands in demurral. "Don't forget—she was black."

"Black!" Zena cried. "You turned her away for racial—"

"No!" Gus said. "I'm no racist, and neither is Thatch. Especially not about young women. But she must have seen our white skins and been afraid. No way she'd set foot inside this bus! If I were a white girl invited aboard with three black men, I'd feel the same."

"Race never entered my mind," Gordon said. "But your point is well taken. Even Gloria would hesitate. In retrospect, I think we are guilty. We should have reassured her, or tried to."

"We'll lose time," Gus said. "We could all drown!"

But the vote was now two to two. Gus pondered a moment, then capitulated. "All right, Thatch. They'll just have to learn the hard way."

Obediently, Thatch turned. They made their way back in silence.

It was difficult to locate the precise spot where they had left the girl, because the interstate was largely featureless in the rain. They cruised for thirty-five minutes—more than far enough—but didn't see any figure on the street. The pouring rain and thickening fog made a wider search impossible. The girl was gone.

"She could have flagged us down, if she had wanted to," Gordon said.

Gus was disgusted. "All that time and gas wasted. And the water getting deeper all the time. We could have used the break to forage for caulking materials, too. Are you satisfied now?"

"At least we tried," Zena said. "We aren't savages." But over an hour had been wasted, which meant another inch of rain and possibly another six inches of channelized flooding. Had she prejudiced their own chances by her foolish quest?

"Have we passed the Suwannee River yet?" Gordon inquired.

"No," Gus replied. "Why the hell do you think I'm in such a hurry?"

That hardly helped Zena's conscience. The worst flooding would be in the Suwannee River valley, naturally—no peaceful stream of folklore and song today!

They moved on north, glumly. One hour, two hours, slowly because of the deteriorating visibility. Gus began to hum "Way down upon the Suwannee River ..." and it was all Zena could do to resist the baiting. She began to nod again—and the bus slowed.

Flooding again? She held her breath. No, Thatch had spotted another person. A woman in a yellow cape, trying futilely to fix the motor of her car.

"I'll talk to her!" Zena cried. "You men keep your big mouths shut!"

Gordon smiled, Gus frowned, and Thatch seemed to be indifferent. Zena got out, ignoring the harsh beat of water on her head, hair, and third set of dry clothes, and approached the woman. She felt like a procurer, and it made her sick. But the alternative—

"We have a man who might be able to start it for you," Zena called.

The woman faced her, the fine lines of her face set off by the fringe of rain-bedraggled hair outside her rain cape. "It's out of gas and the battery's dead. I just wanted you to know I was in trouble. I waited in the car for hours, knowing the highway had been closed to traffic, hoping—until I heard you come. Are you a rescue vehicle?"

"No such luck," Zena said. "But we'll help you."

"You saved my life!"

For a fate worse than death? "Look, we're a party of

four, at the moment. Three men—and one of them seems to have notions of picking up grateful girls. You know. I hit him, and I think he's harmless. But with this flooding—we may be trapped together for days."

"Nothing could be worse for me than being trapped here."

"That's what *I* thought. But—"

"I don't think this rain is ever going to end!"

"Not soon, I'm afraid. We've already passed through serious flooding, and the worst is coming. Frankly, I think you'd better hitch a ride with us. I just wanted you to know—"

"I understand. There won't be any trouble. Usually I travel with my husband, but he's in California right now. I don't think you appreciate how grateful I am for the chance to get moving again."

"You don't have to be grateful—but it will help if you pull your weight. We're all dead tired from hauling this tonnage out of a flooded section."

"I understand," the woman repeated firmly. "I'm Karen Jimson."

"Zena Emers." They shook hands formally, while the rain beat down on both their heads. "Let's get the heck inside!"

They went up to the bus and climbed in. "Karen, this is Gus, Thatch, Gordon," Zena introduced. "Men, this is Mrs. Jimson. She's out of gas, so will ride with us—until the rain stops."

Karen nodded in turn to each of the men. The light of the interior and the clinging wetness of her clothes under the cape showed her to be a young, buxom girl, not quite running to fat. "I have to fetch some things from the car," she said.

"Married!" Gus expostulated the moment Karen was out of earshot.

"Why, whatever difference does that make?" Zena inquired sweetly.

Soon Karen was back with two small suitcases. "We're all tired," Gordon said. "Why don't we park here and sleep? I can start the motor in the morning—and delay is better than cracking into something from fatigue. Thatch hasn't had a break since we started, has he?"

"I don't think we'd better stop," Zena said, still conscious of the delay she had caused. "The water is still rising."

"Then let me drive," Gordon said. "Thatch has to have relief."

Even Gus had to agree to that. "You girls take the back bunks," he said. "A bed pulls down above the driving compartment, but we can't use that while we're in motion. Thatch and I can use the dining alcove."

There was no protest. The men folded down the alcove-bed, and Zena closed off the rear section, forming it into a room. She stripped, dumped the dripping things in the sink on top of the last batch, found an oversized negligee in the female closet, donned it, and lay down. She expected sleep to come rapidly, but instead she lay tired and awake.

Karen removed her wet garments more slowly. Zena had not meant to snoop, but couldn't resist. Karen's figure, unlike Gloria's, was genuine; she was a well-fleshed woman.

Karen opened one of her suitcases and removed something. Zena could not make out what it was. The woman leaned over, did something, and finally straightened.

Then Zena saw the needle. Karen had injected something into her own thigh.

Zena felt a throb of dismay. Karen had seemed like an ideal prospect for the long haul: sensible, well-adjusted, handsome. Obviously she wasn't. Drug addiction would be an overwhelming liability in this situation!

Should she tell the others? No, that would do no good, and the truth would surely emerge in its own course. Besides, she didn't want to admit she had been peeking.

How much misery and crime was allowed to flourish unchallenged in the world, she wondered, because of the silence of hypocrites like herself? Perhaps it was best that it all be washed out by the deluge. She knew she would have a bad night—but instead she slept soundly throughout.

The bus stopped in the early gloom, waking everyone. Gordon turned off the motor and stood, stretching. "I'm hungry," he said.

Gus, sleepy, started to protest the delay, then saw what lay ahead. A broad lake obviously too deep to drive through. The Suwannee was at hand!

"I've done my stint," Gordon said as he raided the refrigerator. "No sense wasting gas, which is already low. We're stranded for the time being."

He did not really believe in the permanency of the rain, Zena remembered. No sense arguing.

"Thatch, do something!" Gus cried. *Gus* believed!

Thatch peered about. "No anchorages for pulleys," he said. "I'm afraid this is it. We'll just have to swim."

A fair assessment, Zena thought. The bus had been nice, very nice, but they couldn't stay in that cocoon forever while the water rose.

"Get this machine across!" Gus shouted. His volume made the others wince. He seemed to be afraid.

Thatch looked at him helplessly. "If I try to drive it there, it'll stall."

"Why should it? We caulked it."

Now Zena remembered: there had been a stop in the night, and some getting out and working. She had heard it, but no one had called her to help and she had been too logy to rise on her own initiative. Thatch and Gordon must have sealed the crevices and panels, or tried to.

"That may keep the water out of the residential sec-

48

tion," Gordon said. "But not out of the motor. It will stall."

"Maybe it will, maybe it won't," Gus said angrily. "Drive, Thatch."

Thatch shrugged and got into the driver's seat.

"This is crazy!" Zena said. "It's useless to—"

The motor started. Thatch drove the vehicle into the water. Zena held her breath, knowing what was going to happen.

But the water was more shallow than it had looked. The bus continued, making enormous splashes to either side. The shore line receded behind, fifty feet, seventy-five, a hundred.

Zena let out her breath. And the motor stalled.

"Now you've done it!" Gus said angrily to Thatch.

Zena wanted to yell at Gus, but sighed instead. Yelling might be satisfying, but it would not solve any problems.

Gordon finished his breakfast and went to the bathroom. "I'm going to sleep," he announced.

Karen looked about. "Is there anything I can take that floats? I can't swim."

"You won't have to swim!" Gus said. "We're getting this thing across. Time to start pushing, Thatch."

"We can't push it that far," Zena objected. "We tried that before."

"You can *start*," Gus said. "It's still downhill, some. Get moving, Thatch."

"Get moving, Thatch!" Zena mimicked. "For God's sake, Gus, downhill means deeper into the water!"

"We can still push," Karen said. "I'll help. But let's eat first."

"There's not much food," Zena said, remembering the woman's injection of the prior evening. Was Karen in a drug euphoria? "And we don't want to waste it." Actually, she hadn't resented Gordon's meal. He was an asset to the group; was Karen?

But Karen had found some wrapped lumps of sugar. She opened them and ate them quickly.

They took turns using the little bathroom, where Zena's several sets of soggy clothing remained in the sink. The closet supply would not last forever; they would have to find a way to dry things. "Don't flush the toilet," Zena warned. "We may need the water. We can't trust what's outside."

Karen went back to the bedroom. "Oh!" she said.

Zena came to look. Gloria had remanifested, and was asleep on the couch Karen had used.

"That's Gordon's other self," Zena explained. "He says he is a woman in a male body."

"He seemed perfectly sensible to me," Karen said, shaken. "I never guessed he was—"

"He *isn't*. Just let him be. *Her* be. We all have our little secrets."

Karen looked quickly at her, seeming to comprehend in that moment that Zena knew about her addiction. But she did not speak again.

They went out into the rain-blasted lake: Thatch and Karen and Zena. By common consent they left Gloria to sleep; he/she had done his/her part by driving at night. Gus, of course, was a hopeless case; the girls could not have dragged him out, and Thatch would not.

It *was* downhill. They pushed, and the bus moved, slowly. And the water deepened, climbing Zena's thighs. The rain lanced down, as ever.

Zena knew it couldn't last. They would soon be exhausted, and it would be impossible to get the bus up out of the water without using the pulley system. And impossible to use the pulleys without anchorages. Also, the increasing depth of the water was making things extremely awkward.

They stopped to rest, gasping. "Why do I go along with this idiocy?" Zena asked rhetorically. She was waist-deep now and more than physically weary.

"Why didn't you wake me?"

"What?" Zena looked about, confused. But it had not been Thatch speaking. Gordon had joined them.

"We didn't see you," Karen said. "There was only some blonde. . . ."

Gordon grinned. They got together and pushed again, making slightly better progress now that they were four. The water was up to Zena's shoulders and the whole of the vehicle's chassis was beneath the troubled surface. They would never get it out of this!

"Stop," Gordon said.

Zena stopped pushing, glad to get her chin out of the waves. But the bus continued moving. Thatch and Karen also stood back.

They stared as it proceeded without them.

"I was afraid of that," Gordon said. "The current's taken it. We have lost control."

"Current?" Zena felt stupid, perhaps from fatigue. But of course there was a current! All this water was in transit, flowing from high ground to low ground. The bus presented a broad expanse of surface to intercept that force, now that the main body of it was in the water. A much more powerful push than three tired people could produce—or combat.

"The brakes!" Gordon cried, "Gus, put on the brakes!" But it was hardly likely that Gus could hear.

Zena forged up to the front, finding relief in full swimming but barely exceeding the bus's velocity. She realized that Karen was being quite brave, if she really couldn't swim, for at the rate they were going the water would soon be over her head.

"Gus—brakes!" Zena cried.

Now Gus heard. "You've got her going well! Don't quit now!"

"We're not doing it! The current—"

"Current!" Gus looked out the window, alarmed.

The bus kept moving. "Put on the brakes!" Zena screamed.

"I did!" Gus screamed back. "They're locked!"

"They can't be. It's going faster than ever!"

Then, slowly, she realized. The brakes were not working, because the entire vehicle was floating!

Slowly, ponderously, like a runaway but clumsy barge, the bus wallowed in the current, going where the water took it. Zena just stood there and stared, bemused. Thatch and Gordon came into view on the other side, mouths open. Karen stood a little farther back.

Zena began to laugh, hysterically. Karen joined her. In a moment Gordon laughed too—a girlish titter. The incongruity of that set Zena off worse, though she understood the reason for that falsetto. Gloria was the dominant personality, when it came to falling apart.

Thatch merely shook his head.

The bus began to drift sidewise, off the highway.

"Thatch, *do* something!" Gus's voice came back despairingly. "It's coming in the engine hatch!"

"Well, sit on the hatch!" Gordon shouted. "Hold it down, or the whole thing will sink!"

"Maybe 'capsize' is the word," Zena said, fending off another attack of the hopeless giggles.

Thatch swam after the bus.

"No way to stop it," Gordon said. "It'll float right on out to sea."

But fate intervened again. Before Thatch caught up, the bus snagged on something under the surface, rotated in a quarter circle, and hung there, bobbing gently. It was off the highway, but no longer drifting with the current.

They came up to it again, four heads showing above murky water. "Thatch, I told you to get this bus across!" Gus called irritably from the interior. He was still sitting on the engine cover between the front chairs.

Zena quelled another flash of emotion: rage or mirth, or both. She knew she was overreacting. Was the man totally impervious to reason? "I'm sure he is doing his best," she said, with what irony she was not certain herself.

Thatch considered, then swam away. The others clung to the bus uncertainly. Zena didn't have the gumption to challenge Thatch on where he was going; it could be a plan to save the motor-home, or merely a call of nature.

"Well, let's get inside for now," Gordon said.

They splashed around to the door, Gordon helping Karen, who looked wan. Zena reached it first—and met another aggravation. It would not open.

"Gus, don't be childish!" she cried, exasperated.

But Gordon fathomed the problem. "It's not him, it's the water. The pressure's holding it shut."

"And if we do yank it open," Karen pointed out, "all the water will pour inside and sink the ship."

Zena laid her head against the metal. "What are we going to do?"

"Use the window," Gordon said. "That's how I came out. I'll boost you up."

Karen went first, wriggling through with Gordon supporting her fleshy legs and Gus getting whatever grip he could on her robust upper torso. Watching that, Zena had second thoughts about her mode of entry. "You go next," she said to Gordon. "Then *you* can help me in from inside."

Gordon didn't need boosting. For all his effeminate preferences, he was a well-conditioned man. He hauled himself up and through with minimum trouble.

Still, Zena lingered. "We're forgetting Thatch! Maybe I should wait here—"

"Suit yourself," Gordon said amenably. "But if you get cold, I'll spell you." He looked about inside. "We'll have to do some bailing; that engine cover's still leaking. Karen, why don't you perch on it, and I'll find a bucket . . ."

Zena was cold, but didn't care to admit it. They waited, more or less helplessly. Buckets of water flew out the window to merge with the rain: Gordon was at work.

In due course Thatch returned. He bore several long poles that he had evidently fashioned from saplings.

53

"Oars!" Zena cried, comprehending.

"We still have to carve them flat," Thatch said. "But they won't fit inside."

"Well, do it outside!" Gus snapped from the window.

"Why don't you come out and do it yourself?" Zena snapped back.

Gus looked down at her, amazed. "And get wet?"

She thought he was joking then realized with a sick feeling that he was not. They might all drown for lack of manpower, but big Gus would not get wet.

Zena shrugged and looked at Thatch. "Have another knife?"

He did. First they had to float the poles back to shore, where they could be worked on. This was simply a matter of supporting the forepart of one's body on the wood and kicking the feet. It was against the current, but not too difficult.

The air, as she came back into it from her submersion, seemed chill. Was the rain cooling, or was it just her? She hoped she wasn't coming down with any illness. That would be all they needed now: a contagious disease.

They worked on the oars side by side, sitting astride them and pushing the kitchen knives away two-handed. It was awkward, but seemed to get the job done with minimum risk. A bad slip, a gash across the wrist—that could be fatal!

But she was growing unnecessarily morbid, looking for pretexts to feel sorry for herself, when there were plenty of real problems to occupy her attention!

"Thatch," she murmured, suspecting that he would not hear her through the beat of rain, and half hoping for that.

"Yes?" he replied.

All right: out with it! "Karen—I saw her inject herself with something last night."

He paused. "I'd better tell Gus."

"No, you idiot! What use would he be?"

54

"He knows what to do."

"What is it with you two?" she cried. "You do all the work. He's nothing but a parasite."

"He does his part."

"His part! What's his part? Conspicuous consumer?"

"He leads."

"Some leadership! He won't even poke his nose outside."

"Well, it's wet outside."

"Oh come on now, Thatch!"

He didn't answer, and she didn't push it. When the knife began to dull Thatch showed her how to sharpen it with a little whetstone he had, and the laborious work continued.

When they had four oars, they got up. Zena's hands were cramped and hurting; there would be blisters. Now for the swim back.

"About time!" Gus called as they drew alongside.

"Don't you know that every hour makes it worse? We have to reach high ground."

"We can put the oars through the windows, and row," Thatch said. "It won't matter how deep the water gets."

"You have no anchorages in the windows," Gus said.

Zena was fleetingly amused to see how the normal roles of the two men had reversed. Now Gus was protesting while Thatch gave answers.

"I'll take care of that," Gordon said. "I've been considering the layout. We'll have to nail some blocks in."

"Then we can't close the windows!" Gus said. "The rain will come in."

So that was it: Gus was really concerned about his personal comfort. True to form after all!

"I'll remove the blocks once we're back on land," Gordon said. "It'll get wet in here—but that's the least of evils."

"The rugs! The furniture!" Gus exclaimed.

Gordon ignored him. "Pass in an oar handle, folks, so I can piece this out. We need room for the oarsmen, too."

"There are no blocks," Gus said.

"We'll have to cut some lengths off the ends of the oars," Gordon said.

They had no saw, so had to carve off segments with the knives. Thatch was good at this, though Zena saw that his hands were badly blistered; he had cut down the trees this way, too. More time was lost, while the rain rained. Zena was afraid the bus would float off its impediment before they were ready. She decided not to voice this thought, however. What could they do about it except worry?

But the water level now seemed to be constant, though the rain never abated. Apparently the broad flow sufficed to keep it stable, here—for the time being. Gordon, with much hammering and unladylike swearing, got the makeshift apparatus done.

At last they were ready for the big effort. Gordon helped Zena in, and Thatch stayed outside to make sure the oars were functioning correctly. Zena and Karen had the rear pair; they braced their feet against the back panel of the bus and sat facing rearward on the two side couches, holding on to the heavy awkward oar handles. Gus had the dinette-alcove oar; he was seated similarly on the bed set there. Gordon stopped bailing, set a box of shoes, wet clothing and other artifacts on the engine panel to help hold it down, and took the kitchen oar. He had the hall to move in.

"Now push down and forward on your oars," Thatch called from behind. "That lifts them up and forward, outside."

Zena tried. It was like wrestling a rigid snake. The leverage was all against her.

She wasn't the only one; Karen was struggling valiantly to master her oar, and finally got it pinned under her body. A banging up front indicated that at least one of the men was having trouble too.

"Get them together!" Thatch shouted. "Otherwise the craft will spin about."

But Zena could not manage her oar, let alone coordinate it with anyone else's.

"No, no, it's all wrong!" Thatch cried.

"Come in here and take my oar," Gus called. "*I'll* show you how to organize."

Thatch swam up and climbed in the window, while Gordon bailed some more. There was a constant inflow of water from somewhere, despite the patching and caulking, and the rug was covered an inch deep. The two men changed places. Then Gus strode down the hall and perched on the rear couch with his feet clear of the water. He faced forward between the two girls.

"Take your places," he cried. "Now everybody push down." His voice carried better than Thatch's and had a greater imperative. Zena found herself responding with extra effort despite her resentment. Trust Gus to land the softest spot!

"Karen, get your hands on it, not your chest," Gus continued. "Gordon, don't move it yet—just hold it in place. You're stronger than the girls, so you'll have to hold back a little. Now, when I call 'Forward,' I want you all to push your oars toward me, together—but keep those handles down! Okay—now *forward!*"

They shoved their unwieldy handles forward. Under his direction they let the handles rise, so that the paddle ends dropped more or less neatly into the water outside. No splash was audible through the steady noise of the rain, but Zena felt the change in balance. "Now, pull back, hard!"

They pulled together, and the bus lurched free of its encumbrance. It tilted and wallowed alarmingly, then steadied. Zena hoped she would not be seasick.

"Now we're on the high seas," Gus said, unperturbed. "Keep those oars moving! Down—forward—up *pull!*"

Zena obeyed almost mindlessly, and felt the bus begin to move. They were doing it—they were rowing it across the water!

And it was idle Gus who had accomplished that final unified action, not Thatch or anyone else. Gus had after all emerged as the leader when it counted. Thatch had tried, but failed: he had neither the voice nor the talent to organize people. In performance, Thatch was a loner.

The rowing became easier as they got the hang of it, though it was cruelly tiring. Zena's arms were soon numb with fatigue, but Gus kept the cadence going and she didn't dare be the first to stop.

Then Karen collapsed over her oar. "Halt!" Gus bawled. "Gordon, start bailing before we sink! The rest of you rest in place, catch your breath. We're nearing land; one more drive will do it."

Thank God, Zena thought. For the rest and for the sight of the end. She had never before labored so hard.

Then they resumed, and it was as bad as before. Karen had recovered enough to pull her oar, but Zena could tell they were not making the progress they had been. The current of the water and the sheer weight of the bus were too much.

Suddenly the engine cover burst its latches. Water gushed in, carrying away the box and flooding the interior. The bus began to sink.

"Keep paddling!" Gus cried.

Then they ran aground. The vehicle seemed to bounce slightly as the wheels touched bottom. The water continued to climb inside, but Zena knew they would not drown.

"Keep rowing!" Gus yelled. "I'll steer!" He got down and waded up the hall to the driver's seat.

However, the rowing was now ineffective. Gus set the brakes and they relaxed, dead-armed. They had made it, after a fashion.

Now the rain seemed extra loud, though it had never abated. Zena wondered why. Perhaps this was because she had been out in it so long, and then had had to struggle with the oar. For the first time since daybreak, she had nothing to do but listen.

"Is there any sugar?" Karen asked. No one answered.

What a deluge this was! If only they had listened to her, those paramilitary experts of the space station. All this could so readily have been avoided. . . .

"Let's go with the pulleys!" Gus said, sloshing back down the aisle. "The water'll drain once we get out."

Zena sighed. At least he had gotten his feet wet. That was progress of a kind. "Gus, we're worn out!"

"You'll be *drowned* if we don't get on out of here before the deep flooding starts," he responded. "This thing won't float so well next time, now that it's waterlogged. It was sinking the whole time we were paddling."

"*We* were paddling," Zena muttered ironically.

"You can rest once we're driving again."

Wearily they got up and clambered out the front window. Gordon got the pulley apparatus down from the roof-rack while Thatch and Zena surveyed for anchorages. They were in luck: There were several illegal billboards with firm grounding posts. Many things, Zena thought bitterly, were not made the way they used to be, not made to last. Billboards *were*.

The hauling took an interminable time, even though Karen was there to help. But long before it was done, she weakened and had to go back to the bus. "That's the trouble with drug dependency," Zena muttered. "The high gives out, and you're worse off than before."

"Drug addiction!" Gordon exclaimed.

"Yes, I saw her take a shot last night. I don't know what kind."

"That doesn't necessarily make her an addict."

"Why would she hide it, then?"

Gordon didn't answer. The three of them continued hauling.

At last they made it out of the water. They blocked the wheels and trekked around to the door and inside.

Gus and Karen were just rising from what had obviously been an intimate liaison. While the three dead-tired people had labored outside, the two rested ones had indulged in the most basic of entertainments.

"All right, get the motor started!" Gus said, covering up in more ways than one. "Long drive ahead!"

Wearily, Gordon worked on the motor, while Thatch saw to the draining and cleaning of the refrigerator, range and other conveniences. A layer of thin mud was over everything that the water had touched. Zena checked the lashings on the oars, which were now mounted on the roof, and made sure the ropes and pulleys were secure. She was not only worn out, she was sick.

She stood against the back of the bus, face shielded from the rain, and sorted it out. What, specifically, was bothering her? Was it the inequity of allowing three hard workers to carry the load for two shirkers? No, not exactly; Karen had manned an oar and helped for a while with the hauling. She really had been about to drop. Gus had performed a necessary service by calling the cadence for rowing; otherwise they'd be floating yet—perhaps right out to sea. Or worse, they'd be sunk because of that burst engine cover—in twenty feet of dirty water, with one of their number unable to swim. How many of the rest could have bucked the current and made it the long distance to shore?

Was it that Gus had taken advantage, forcing his attentions on a woman too tired to resist? No, Gus was lazy, and self-interested, but hardly that forceful about sex; Karen could have rebuffed him with a word, or failing that, a scream, had she chosen to. Certainly she had made a miraculous recovery of energy! Another shot of her drug?

Was it, then, that Karen was married? That was disturbing—yet really it was her own business. Certainly a married woman knew what it was all about, and could make her own decisions.

What, then? Why should Zena herself be so upset about

a matter that was hardly her affair? She had problems enough of her own to worry about!

Her stomach heaved, but she managed to hold her gorge down. The last thing she wanted to do was waste precious food! Probably she was merely reacting to the strain of overwork and the mind-deadening smash of rain, on and on.

The motor coughed, making her jump, for she was almost astride the tail pipe. Gordon had worked his magic once more and they were about to be on their way—again.

Inside, all was not well. They were low on food, water, and gasoline.

"We've got to get more," Gus said.

"There isn't any more," Thatch replied, sounding querulous. That was another thing: how had this Gus/Karen thing affected Thatch? "No stores or stations will be open in this rain—and we don't have enough money."

"Don't give me that!" Gus snapped. "I tell you we need supplies, not excuses—and within the hour!"

Just like that, Zena thought. Gus was true to form.

"It wouldn't be right to—" Thatch was saying.

"You think anybody's going to care what we take—after it's all underwater?" Gus demanded. "We'd better salvage what we can!"

"He has a point," Gordon said. "I don't approve of theft, but this is hardly a typical circumstance."

Thatch nodded regretfully. "I suppose not."

"Aren't you making a big assumption?" Karen asked. "Pretty soon this rain will stop, and—"

"No. It'll never stop," Gus said. "Not till all this is way underneath. That's why we're driving so hard for the mountains."

The motor was running smoothly now, and Gordon came inside. "Thatch and Zena and I have to collapse," he said. "Gus'd better drive."

Thatch began to shake his head, but Karen cut him off. "I know how to drive."

"Women don't—" Gus began.

"Oh, it will be quite safe," Karen said, "with you to help me."

Gus tried to protest, but she led him to the front. He seemed to be unable to resist her suggestion.

Zena looked at Thatch, but he was already lying on the dinette bed. Then her eye caught Gordon's—and he winked.

Karen could make Gus go along because she had taken the trouble to show him what she could do for him. Smart, smart! Maybe Gordon had suggested the notion to her.

Zena quelled another surge of nausea and flopped wetly on the back couch.

## Chapter 3: Floy

When she woke, it was because the bus was stopping. Gloria was on the parallel couch, still asleep. Once more Zena considered that classic feminine face, that long blonde hair, that artificially full bosom. No matter how tired he was, Gordon alway took time to convert to Gloria for repose!

Why didn't this inversion upset her the way Karen's antics had? Zena didn't know. "Sleep on, sleeping beauty," she murmured, and strode forward.

Thatch, too, remained asleep. Gus and Karen were stretching. "Filling station," Gus said. "Should be gas here—and we're down to under five gallons. Which is not much for a bus this size. Maybe food here too."

"I hope so!" Karen said fervently. She did not look well, but Zena could not tell what was wrong with her. She wished she knew more about drugs.

"We can siphon gas," Gus said, "if we can find a tube."

"Or just pump it out of the pump," Karen said.

"Hey, yes!" he agreed, startled. "I'm thinking too much like a criminal."

At least he felt some twinge of guilt, Zena thought. But so it had to be. No one would have any use for it after this group passed. The sea was rising.

"You look," Gus said. "It's still raining."

"Sorry, I forgot," Zena said sharply. But as usual, the irony was wasted on him.

She went out, hunching momentarily as the water soaked her once more. The rain *was* colder now! If she didn't catch pneumonia. . . .

Karen followed her, hunching similarly. "Zena, listen," she called over the noise. "I want to explain—"

"You don't have to explain anything to me."

"You told me at the outset how the men expected—"

"And you told me you were married."

"My husband's in California! Do you think I'll ever see him again?"

That stopped her. California was as good as Mars, as far as accessibility went. If he were not dead already, he might as well be. Karen, therefore, was being practical. Still, that drug addiction—"We have gas and food to find," Zena said, moving on.

"Yes, of course! But it is important to encourage everyone to participate—"

Zena opened the glass door and stepped inside. It was true that Karen had gotten Gus to contribute a little more to group survival than he might have otherwise, but that hardly seemed to justify the method.

The place had been ransacked. The floor was covered with debris, and the shelves were empty.

"If it's this bad in a filling station," Zena asked rhetorically, "how bad is it going to be in a supermarket?"

"They missed the candy machine!" Karen said. "Come on!"

64

"I never broke into a machine in my life."

"You may not need candy, but believe me, I *do!*" Karen found a large screwdriver and began prying.

Disgusted, Zena walked out. She checked the pumps in front, but they appeared to be out of gas. It was evident that many people had been alert to the spoils of anarchy—and much faster to act. But they had been hurried, no doubt eager to get home; a careful search should turn up more than candy bars.

There was a noise, not the rain. Zena looked around before remembering that Karen was at work inside the station, probably hammering on the machine. No sense getting jumpy about sounds.

There were elevated tanks behind. Did they hold reserves of gasoline? Or something else? But they sounded hollow under the beat of rains: indication enough.

She came back around the side. A door said MEN. That reminded her: they needed water to flush the toilet—and water to drink, too. They could always collect rain, but if there were running water here for the bus's tanks, that would be easier.

She walked around to the WOMEN door and tried the handle. The door was locked.

There was a banging from inside.

Karen?

Zena walked to the front and peered through the glass. Karen was still working on the machine.

Back at the WOMEN door, Zena knocked. "Are you all right?" she called, feeling a bit foolish.

"Locked in!" a childish treble replied. "Help!"

"You can open it," Zena said. "Pull out the dingus and turn the handle."

"I can't!"

"Just a minute." Zena looked about. After a moment's search she found a curved crowbar lying on the ground, apparently thrown there by the prior vandals. She picked it up and inserted the sharp end into the crack of the door.

Then it became obvious why the lock would not release: the moisture had made it swell tight.

Zena threw her body into it, not concerned about damage. There was a lot of leverage in a crowbar. Something cracked, and she was able to jam the point in deeper. Another heave, and the door pried out, its lock ruined.

A young girl, thirteen or fourteen, was inside. She was dry and rather pretty.

Then a yellow animal attacked. Zena fended it off, batting it away. Her leg stung from a scratch.

"Dust Devil!" the girl exclaimed, stumbling.

It was a little cat. It withdrew, snarling.

The girl swept her hand toward it. She caught the hind end of the cat, and picked up the animal, hauling it into the air by its back legs. "This is Dust Devil," she said. "He's not a bad cat, really. He just doesn't like people."

"If that's how you treat him, no wonder!"

"He understands about me. Who are you?"

"Zena Emers. You?"

"What?"

"Who are you?"

"Oh! Floy. Floy Sanford. And this is Dust Devil. He—"

"Yes, I know," Zena said. "What are you doing in here?"

"Well, I came to—you know—and when I got out, they were gone. I didn't know where to go, so I didn't. Go anywhere. And then the door stuck."

"*Who* was gone? Your family?"

"Yes."

"Did something happen to them?"

"No, they just drove off. I wasn't too surprised, really."

"Drove off and left you—deliberately?"

"It was sort of crowded. They didn't much like Dust Devil."

"*That* I can understand. But still—how long ago?"

"I don't know. It was around midnight, and the rain didn't stop."

"Midnight! Twelve hours ago?"

66

"I guess. I slept some. Got any food?"

"I'm here looking for some! And gasoline."

"Is it still raining?"

Zena, dripping wet before the door that opened out into the endless storm, didn't bother to answer. So this girl was stranded, deserted by her own family. What was to become of her?

"Floy, how old are you?" If she were older than she looked—

"Fourteen. Dust Devil's one year, next week. He doesn't much like people, except me."

No genius, obviously! A fourteen year old girl with her vicious cat—how would that pair fit into Gus's prospective harem?

What choice was there? "Come on," Zena said.

"But it's raining!"

"Do you want to stay here until it floods? We have a motor-home—and if we can just find gas, we'll be driving north to the highlands."

"My folks were going south."

Was it poetic justice, that those who had deserted this child would die in the flood, while Floy herself survived? Zena led the way out. Floy lurched into the doorway, banging against it.

"Watch where you're going! You'll hurt yourself," Zena said sharply.

"I don't hurt easy." Floy shoved outside and took a full sprawl on the soaking pavement.

"For God's sake, girl!" Zena cried, hauling her up by an arm. "Are you sick?" Again that fear of some debilitating disease made her shudder.

"No worse'n usual. Just never was much for moving around."

Now, holding on to Floy, Zena became aware that the girl was moving with extraordinary lack of grace. "What's wrong with you?"

67

"Just clumsy—awful clumsy," Floy said. "Butterfingers all over. Always been this way—but now it's worse."

"Did you suffer nerve damage as a baby?"

"Maybe. I don't know."

It was becoming more apparent why Floy had been left. This child would have been a problem in survival in the best of health. She was a disaster in her present condition.

Zena got Floy into the front office, where Karen had succeeded in breaking open the candy machine. "Sixty-one assorted candy bars!" Karen gloated. "Who is *she*?"

"She was trapped in the john. Name's Floy."

Floy snatched up a candy bar, scattering several others across the floor in the process. "Hey!" Karen yelped. "We *need* those!"

"She hasn't eaten for twelve hours or more," Zena said. "Spare one from your hoard. It isn't as if it's such precious food."

"It's the *vital* food," Karen said.

Zena sighed. What a mishmash of oddballs she traveled with! From what narcotic vision had that dietetic revelation emerged?

There was a feline screech, followed by a human one. Karen shoved something furry away.

"That's Dust Devil," Zena said.

Karen wiped her scratched leg. "So nice to have a formal introduction!"

"We've got to find gasoline," Zena said. "Otherwise, we may never leave here."

"Are you going to take me with you?" Floy asked, sounding indifferent.

"I don't see what choice we have," Zena said, shaking her head. "But first you'll have to understand about—"

"She's only a child!" Karen interrupted her.

"That's why she has to understand."

"Understand what?" Floy asked.

"Never mind." Karen said.

68

"Oh, so we're getting finicky about morality now," Zena said nastily.

"Age of consent," Karen muttered, at a double disadvantage because of her position and the presence of the child.

"What's the age of consent for being deserted in a filling station?"

"What is it you're talking about?" Floy demanded.

"There are five of us," Zena explained, deciding she was being unfair to Karen. There *were* things that should not be discussed too frankly, here. "Six, counting you—and it's going to be crowded and difficult."

"That's all? Story of my life," Floy said. "I thought maybe you had a sex maniac aboard." She walked to the glass window and looked at the streaming water.

Karen stared after her. "Palsy?" she whispered.

Zena shrugged. "Human being."

"I don't like being alone," Floy said. "If I hadn't had Dust Devil—"

"We can't take the cat!" Zena exclaimed.

"That's what I thought. So I guess I'll stay here."

"You can't stay here. In hours it'll flood!"

"Dust Devil's all I have."

Zena sighed again. "Maybe we'll *all* stay, with no gas."

"There must be cars we can siphon it from," Karen said. "Or other stations nearby."

"Yes." Zena shook herself. "There *have* to be."

Karen had gathered all the candy bars into an oily cloth and made a bundle of them. "We'd better go back."

"Wait—someone's coming," Zena said, seeing a tall shape.

It was Gordon. "Why didn't you wake me?"

"Rhetorical question," Zena said. "He always says that. Gordon, meet Floy and Dust Devil."

"Pleased to know you both," Gordon said without hesitation. "You'll be joining our party, of course. Let me carry Dust Devil."

"Careful," Floy warned. "He doesn't much like—"

"Cats and I understand each other," Gordon said, lifting the little feline without protest. "Come, dear—take my arm."

"Gee," Floy said, flattered. She took firm hold of him and walked with much less difficulty.

Zena turned to find Karen already looking at her. Both were amazed. This was a talent Gordon had not had opportunity to show before.

"What are you going to be when you're adult?" Gordon inquired as they stepped into the rain.

"A dancer," Floy confessed shyly.

Zena bit her tongue.

"I know something about dancing," Gordon said. "Have you ever seen the Drunken Sailor's Hornpipe?" He leaned away from her and did an intricate little step, with the cat waving precariously. The whole thing was ludicrous, in this downpour. "Or did you mean ballet?"

"Ballet!" Floy cried, laughing. "You crazy?"

"Only when the wind is north-northwest."

"That's Shakespeare," she said. "You thought I wouldn't know."

"You caught me!" he admitted. "By the way, Floy— we're almost out of gasoline. Do you know where there's another station, close?"

"There's gas right here," Floy said.

Zena shook her head. "Pump's empty, and so are the big tanks out back."

"Under the ground," Floy explained. "Pump won't bring it up because the power's off. I heard them talking about it, through the wall. You have to work it by hand."

Zena clapped her hand to her forehead. Power off—of course! Naturally the pumps weren't operating.

"My dear, you have sharp ears," Gordon said. "Come meet the others. Watch the step, now—it's slippery."

"The guy's a genius," Karen exclaimed as the two disappeared inside the bus. "Kooked, but smart!"

70

Zena continued to stare after them. "He must have empathy. He says he's miscast in his body, and she's handicapped in hers. It's a lesson to me."

It took them more than an hour to break open a pump, decipher the mechanism, and crank the gasoline out by hand. But when it was done, they had eighty gallons of gas in their two tanks, plus sixteen more stashed in assorted cans. Enough to take them well into the mountains, even if they never found another refill. Floy, however accidentally, had already done them an enormous favor, and earned her keep.

Now they were six, plus the cat—and it *was* crowded. The motor-home was designed to accommodate six, but the manufacturer had obviously not intended them all to be confined to it for twenty-four hours a day without relief.

Two were always resting or asleep on the rear couches, and two were always in the seats up front. That left two—and Dust Devil—in limbo, awake and active with nothing to do. The cat seemed to feel that all comfortable furniture was reserved for him, and he was ready to battle for his rights. The flooded sections of the highway were almost a relief.

Zena washed some clothing in the bathroom and hung it over available edges for whatever drying it could manage. Her legs were tired from standing while the bus jolted. But Thatch was sleeping on the dinette-alcove bed. He could have used the one that came down from the ceiling above the rear bed, but Gus didn't like anyone there when he was with Karen. That left Zena the sodden floor.

"I'm awake," Thatch said. "Sit down."

"Thanks." She sank to the edge of the bunk, relieved to get the weight off her feet.

He swung his own feet to the floor. He was dressed, of course; night clothing was pointless in this circumstance.

71

They had fallen into the habit of changing whenever it was necessary to go outside, so that each person had a dry set of clothing waiting inside. Zena had thus seen more of the others than she liked, and shown more of herself. Gus's eyes did not help.

"Some dream!" Thatch said.

"Dream?" He seldom volunteered anything, and it had not occurred to her that he would have dreams. Now she was curious.

"That I was home with my family," he said.

"There's nothing wrong with that."

"I don't *have* a family. Never did. Only foster homes."

"You were an orphan?"

"Not exactly. Illegitimate."

She found herself both gratified and upset by this confidence. She was glad he now felt free to talk about himself, but appalled at the bleakness of his background. Still, it helped her to understand him. He had never had a normal family, no real roots. Thus, never a chance to develop the sense of security or interdependence of a family relationship.

Gus must have become that family. Dictatorial Gus, like an arrogant father, giving orders that were not to be gainsaid. Yet Gus was weak, too—like some fathers—and that side of him brought out Thatch's loyalty. Thatch's entire lost childhood, the good and the bad, given a twisted fulfillment through this odd subservience.

So she had a comprehension of the man, of sorts. Still, it twisted something in her gut. What was comprehensible was not necessarily acceptable.

Thatch misunderstood her silence. "I did have a father. I just never knew who he was, so I never missed him. And my mother—"

Zena sat up straight. "Mother!" she exclaimed.

Thatch looked perplexed. "Something wrong?"

"What have I been thinking of? My mother lives on the coast!"

72

"So does mine," Gordon said from the driver's seat. Zena had forgotten that he and Floy were within hearing. They had not been snooping; it was almost impossible to hold a private conversation here.

"This flooding—" Zena said.

Gordon slowed the vehicle, so that he could pay more attention to the conversation. That was one of the little ways he showed his priorities. People always came first. "Do you think the sea itself will rise? I assumed that there was only a limited amount of water available to circulate, so that it had to be rising into the atmosphere from the ocean as fast as it falls on land. When this disturbance passes—"

Zena sidestepped that. "The runoff will wash right through the coastal cities. Supplies will be cut. There'll be looting. I want to get my mother *out* of there!"

"I see your point. Where is she?"

"Jacksonville. It's almost on our route."

"My folks are in Norfolk."

"Maybe we couldn't drive all the way in, but we could get close enough to hike the rest of the way," she said eagerly. "Fetch her out—she's a widow, my father died two years ago."

"What nonsense is this?" Gus demanded, coming up from the back room.

"With all our driving problems," Gordon said, "we never thought of other people. Our relatives—"

"We can't go looking for relatives!" Gus exclaimed. "We've got six here now—a full crew!"

"My mother will die, alone in that city!" Zena cried.

"*What* city?"

"Jacksonville."

"We're past Jacksonville! Can't turn back now."

"What?" Zena asked. "We can't be."

"You think we've been standing still while you've been sleeping? The intersection for Jacksonville was at the

73

Suwannee crossing, where we rowed the bus. We're in Georgia now."

"We can't be that far along," Zena said. "There are other roads—"

Karen came up. "She's got a point, Gus. We have to make a side trip for food supplies, too."

Why was food always on Karen's mind, especially sweet food? If she really had that big a hunger, she should weigh two hundred pounds, Zena thought resentfully.

"If we go wandering into flooded cities, we'll never make it to high ground!" Gus said. "We have to save ourselves; we can't do any more than that—but we could do a hell of a lot less than that by diverting our energy and wasting time."

"Do you call saving lives wasting time?" Zena cried, beginning to sound distressingly hysterical in her own ears.

"How many people live in Jacksonville?" Gus demanded. "A million? You want to save one old woman and let the rest wash out to sea?"

"That's heartless!" Zena said, feeling tears in her eyes. She saw Karen nodding, and felt a surge of gratitude for that silent support. After the way she had spoken to Karen, and thought about her. . . .

"No, it's practical," Gus said. "We can't save the world; we can't save even a fraction of it. If we load ourselves down with useless people, we won't even save ourselves."

"Useless people!" Zena cried. "You mean anyone who won't haul on a pulley or serve as a sex object?"

"No!" Gus said, growing heated. Then he paused. "But looking at it your way, maybe the answer is yes."

"*My* way!"

"Now we're fighting among ourselves," Gordon said. "Believe it or not, I can see both sides—and both have merit."

"*What* both sides?" Zena demanded. Her body was shaking.

"His side: we have to get to high ground as rapidly as

74

possible, so we can park without danger of getting flooded out, and can begin foraging for survival supplies. We can't delay even a day, because that might get us trapped behind deep water and an impassable current. And all our members have to be young and healthy, or the group will be too weak to stand up."

"Good summary," Gus agreed. "This is the second deluge, you know—literally. According to the Annular Theory—"

"We aren't all strong or healthy," Zena began. But even in the heat of argument she couldn't speak the obvious about Karen and Floy.

"Your side," Gordon continued, turning to Zena. "Survival of this small group is no good if it is accomplished at the price of dehumanization. We can't preserve our bit of civilization by ruthlessly writing off relatives and ignoring the plight of those most in need. And somewhere in Jacksonville there are bound to be supplies that we shall need for the long haul."

"That's it!" Zena exclaimed. "You think just like a woman."

"Thank you," Gordon said. "Hardly surprising, since I *am* a—"

"Don't start that again, either!" Gus cried.

Gordon paused, and it was almost as though his lip curled. "I propose a compromise. We head for Jacksonville—but only if the road is open and unflooded. If we make it there, we search for Zena's mother. If we can't find her within six hours, we give it up. We give up *all* relatives—mine included."

"But that—" Gus started, realizing the scope of the compromise.

"Put it to a vote," Gordon said. "We're a democracy, aren't we? Maybe it was something else when it started, but everybody has something to contribute to our survival and so everyone has a fair say."

Gus wanted to protest that too, but Karen put her hand

75

on his arm. "I think that's fair, don't you?" she murmured to him.

Gus glanced at her, obviously unwilling to set her against him. Again, Zena felt that turn in her stomach. What means was Karen using to achieve what ends? Was she trying to help the group, or Zena—or herself?

"I proposed the vote, so I'll exclude myself," Gordon said. "Ladies first. Floy?"

"Gee—" Floy began, flattered at the designation.

"Oh, go ahead and see Jacksonville!" Gus said. "But you're making the same mistake as before."

That was another strike at Zena: the lost hour when they had searched in vain for the black girl.

"I'll turn east at the next interchange," Gordon said. "We'll find it."

The chance came within two miles. Gordon turned, and they were soon on a two-lane road. There were traffic lights here, but all were dead, and there was no other traffic. Gordon drove on through without pausing.

Then they approached a city or town: no road signs remained visible, but stalled cars blocked the road, forcing maneuvering. Zena peered through window and rain at the buildings, and thought she saw faces peering back at her. Children's faces, but not animated. The effect was eerie.

"Look at that!" Floy cried, pointing ahead.

It was a store, a supermarket—and it was burning. The rain stifled the flames outside, but the interior was gutted. Several shapes lay before the broken glass frontage. They resembled human bodies.

"There must have been a battle royal," Gus said. "They got hungry and fought over food—and now it's all gone up in flames."

"None left for us," Floy said wistfully.

A man ran out before the bus, waving his arms in the air. Gordon slewed to avoid him, then gunned the motor. They heard a faint shout over the rain-beat—and saw other figures emerge from buildings ahead.

76

"Suddenly I don't like this!" Gordon said. "They're crazed—and if we stop, they'll get aboard—and we may not get moving again."

Glass shattered. Then they heard the sound of the gun. Someone had shot out the kitchen window.

"Turn around!" Gus screamed. "Get us out of here—before they hit the motor or tires!"

Abruptly Zena saw the utter futility of her effort. They had hardly come five miles toward Jacksonville, and already they were under fire. They could never make it—and the chances were that her mother, trapped in a worse area than this because of the denser population and lower terrain, was dead already.

Gordon turned the bus around, skidding on the slick pavement. Figures were all around them, brandishing sticks and pistols. Gordon backed up rapidly, and there was a bang and a scream. He plunged forward—and another figure went down. The bus jerked violently, first the front, then the rear.

Zena clawed her way toward the bathroom, but didn't make it. She vomited on the hall rug.

Now Gordon was speeding well above the safe rate, back through the half-living town, one hand on the horn almost continuously. "Gloria could cry," he muttered wistfully.

"To think," Karen said as she hung on to the kitchen sink, "that this was once a typical, peaceful, conservative suburban community—three days ago."

A hand came down to help Zena up. It was Gus. "I didn't mean it to be like this," he said. Then he lurched into the bathroom and spewed the content of his own stomach into the little sink.

Zena understood.


Miraculously they escaped with no worse damage than the broken window. Thatch put cloth across it, and they resumed travel on the comparatively safe interstate. They had won through to higher ground. The dancing lakes of the lowlands were replaced by the ugly erosion of the slopes. And mischief of another nature.

Gordon was driving again, Floy keeping him company. They had settled into shifts: Gus and Karen, Gordon and Floy, Thatch and Zena. Night was coming, though this made less difference in the rain than it would have ordinarily. At the moment the non-driving shifts were confused, for Gus and Thatch were snoozing at the rear. Zena was playing honeymoon bridge with Karen in the alcove.

"One diamond," Zena bid, considering her dummy.

"One h—" Karen responded as a tire blew out.

The bus lurched. Gordon had been doing twenty-five, his maximum safe speed in the rain. But as the vehicle slewed about, it seemed like seventy.

A second tire blew. The bus bumped to a halt.

"Something in the road," Gordon said. "Glass or nails—had to happen sometime. We've been lucky until now."

"You're too damn philosophical!" Floy complained. "If you aren't going to swear, do you mind if I do?"

Gus and Thatch came up, single file. "Blowout?" Thatch asked. "I can fix it."

"No you don't!" Gus said. The others looked at him. Was Gus actually volunteering?

"Think it through," Gus continued. "Glass from an accident—and no dead cars in the road? Why didn't the rain wash it out?"

"We don't know it's glass," Zena said.

"All the same, don't go out there till we're sure!"

"How can we be sure what it is without looking first?" Floy asked.

"Not what, *who*!"

"It's a paranoid suspicion," Zena said. "We haven't seen any other people since—"

"Since this morning," Karen said.

"Find weapons," Gus said. "We've got hammers, screw-drivers—"

"I'll change those tires myself," Zena cried, disgusted. Gus would rather invent fantastic outside conspiracies than face the prospect of work. She stepped down and pushed open the door.

A heavy hand fell on her shoulder, hauling her into the night. She screamed. Another hand clamped over her mouth. She bit it.

Then it was a wild nocturnal struggle. She threw some-one over her shoulder, but was borne down by another. Figures tumbled out of the door.

There was a snarl, whether animal or human she could not guess. A man screamed, horribly. Zena's attacker jerked away and ran off through the rain.

Zena stood. Another shape loomed, framed by the lights of the bus. She settled into a defensive posture.

"Zena?" It was Gordon's voice.

Her body suddenly felt weak. "Yes! Are the others—?"

"Yes. Only Floy and I came out. Didn't want to risk fighting among ourselves. I think there were only two ambushers. You're quite a scrapper!"

"I was terrified! You drove them off."

"Not I," he said. "Gloria wields a wicked hatpin, but I use my fist—and that scream came before I could mix in."

A yellow streak went up the steps and under the dinette table. "Dust Devil!" Zena said, comprehending the scream. "What an ally in a night fight!" She followed the cat in to see what it carried. The object was small and whitish under the blood. "Oh-oh!"

"Let me see that!" Gordon said, putting his hand on the cat. "My God!"

"What *is* it?" Karen demanded.

"An eyeball," Gordon said.

"Nonsense! That little creature couldn't have—" She paused looking at Floy. The girl was licking off her fingers.

79

"Let's get those tires fixed before the ambushers come back," Gus said. "You see, I was right."

Thatch already had a wrench. He went to the front.

"And post a guard!" Gus said.

"I'll stand guard," Zena said.

"Better be a man," Gus said. "One look at your silhouette and they'll jump you."

"Leave my silhouette out of this!" Zena snapped, realizing that her shirt had been torn in the fray. "But I don't think they'll be back."

Gordon came up with a broom. "I want to be sure that road is clean."

Zena could tell just by walking that nails were scattered across the highway. This had been an ambush, all right. Probably the men had slept nearby, waiting for the sound of blowouts. Lucky they hadn't had guns.

Gordon came up to her. "Take this," he said, putting something into her hand. It was a hatpin—the wickedest she had ever held. The point was super-sharp, and the thing was a good eight inches long.

"Remind me never to fight with Gloria!" she said.

"Don't fight with Floy either," he murmured. "I believe her coordination improves when she acts instinctively—and she has a killer instinct, same as that cat." He moved on, carefully sweeping the wet pavement.

*Yes indeed*, she thought. Innocent, clumsy little Floy—and a scream in the night, part beast, part human agony. A girl licking off her fingers, and a cat chewing contentedly on an eyeball. That pair could take care of themselves.

Gloria, too, with her murderous hatpin. How quickly the predator manifested in adversity!

But she had to give Gus credit too. He had been the first to suspect the ambush. And the first to gird for an indefinite rain, by setting up with the bus and heading for high ground. And he had been right twice about the perils of turning back—for any reason. He had his faults, which were colossal—but he also possessed those devious qualities of leadership and foresight necessary to form this group and get it to safety in time.

In fact, this ill-matched little party might be destined for survival after all.

It looked as though Thatch were finishing up, so she went over. "Did you speak to Gus about Karen?" she asked.

"Yes." He knocked a nut tight and stood up, pocketing a patching kit. It must have been quite a repair job under these conditions, yet he had not complained.

"And?"

"He said he'd take care of it."

"What does he know about drug addiction? Have you seen how lethargic she gets? And this darn preoccupation with sweets. If he lets her off, there's no telling what will happen in the next emergency."

"He knows what to do."

"Why don't *you* ever know what to do, Thatch? Your brain is as good as his."

"No. I never went to college."

"That's irrelevant! Look how you fixed these tires."

Thatch shrugged and started to walk toward Gordon, who was now detectable only by the continuous sounds of sweeping.

"You do all the work," Zena continued, pacing him. "While he—didn't you see what he and Karen were up to, last time we used the pulleys?" That reminded her of another thing. "What steps do you think he'll take to stop her drugs, when she's giving him *that*?"

But Thatch didn't answer, and she felt cheap. He didn't need her to aggravate the situation!

They came up to Gordon. "I think it's clear, now," Gordon said. "Most of the nails are behind us, anyway, and there won't be more traffic along this stretch. I just wanted to be extra sure."

Thatch nodded, and the three started back. "I'm really

beginning to believe that this rain will never stop," Gordon said. "I know some of you have maintained that fact all along, but you can't blame me for being skeptical. I got to thinking, while I swept—if it doesn't stop, and if civilization is wiped out—we may be stuck with each other for a long time."

Zena wanted to comment, but didn't dare. Gordon was coming to grips with the reality. Thatch hadn't been asked a direct question, so he did not respond.

"In that case," Gordon continued, "we should have to begin pairing off. That's not so hard for the rest of you; Gus and Karen already have, and the two of you—"

"*What?*" Zena yelped.

"But for me, it's difficult, because I'm in the wrong body."

"Floy's in the wrong body too," Thatch said.

"Yes. So it would seem to be up to you," Gordon said.

"What are you talking about!" Zena exclaimed indignantly.

"Carrying on," Gordon said.

"What does *that* mean?"

But they had reached the bus, and Gordon elected not to elucidate. Zena had to stew by herself.

Inside, Floy had found some food coloring and fixed up green and blue breadcrusts. "It's Dust Devil's birthday," she announced. "He's one year old along about now."

In a moment Gloria appeared from the bathroom. "Happy birthday, DD!" she cried.

With an eyeball for an appetizer, Zena thought. The shape of things to come?

## Chapter 4: Raid

The long drive continued. They stopped and scrounged for food wherever they could, alert for ambushes, but had little further trouble of that nature. Once again a tire blew out, but that turned out to be from a weak patch Thatch had put on. Floy and Dust Devil turned out to be excellent advance guards, for the cat reacted with loud hostility to the presence of any other living creature and the girl had acute perceptions. Gloria did most of the cooking, for she seemed to have a special talent with the dubious items available.

They encountered few other people, and those contacts were wary and hostile. Where had all the rest gone? Zena wondered, but she did not pursue the subject avidly. Most of those trapped in the cities, like her mother—here Zena clamped her teeth down hard and forced herself to continue her train of thought—most of those trapped when the rain started would have left soon, either because of the flooding or because of hunger. Many in the suburbs would have hidden in their houses until the foundations washed out—and they too would have had to eat. With the civilized supply mechanisms in disorder, anarchy would have come very quickly, as they had seen. It was the sheer luck of this party that they had stayed with the interstate despite the flooding that had driven most others away, and that this highway avoided cities. Even those waiting to ambush moving vehicles would have had far richer pickings elsewhere.

Karen was sweating. Zena noticed this, because it was not that hot in the bus. They were not wasting fuel on such luxuries as heat. Nervousness?

"I'm hungry," Karen said.

"You know we have to ration food," Zena replied tiredly. "Nothing till suppertime." As if they didn't have major problems to worry about, instead of minor neurotic hungers!

"There must be something," Karen said, standing up. Then she swayed, and had to catch herself against the table. Zena put out a hand to steady her, and felt a racing pulse. Karen's skin was clammy, and she was pale.

"Is there something you want to tell us?" Zena asked. If this were a drug reaction, how much better to get it out into the open!

"I wish I were home!" Karen said.

"With your husband?"

"Yes. He understands." She shook her head. "But I'll never see him again."

Zena would have tried to reassure her, but knew the very effort would be hypocritical. Better to let the ugly truth stand. Karen was probably a widow already.

Karen sat down again and looked at Zena. She was breathing shallowly. "Sugar," she said.

Zena blew out her breath in disgust. "No sugar!" Here

84

she had thought the woman was suffering an emotional trauma because of separation from her spouse. . . !

"No sugar." Karen echoed faintly.

"What is this thing about sweets?" Zena demanded. "Don't you have more serious concerns than spoiling your teeth?"

"I'm sorry," Karen said. And began trembling.

She just wasn't about to admit she was an addict! Well, maybe she was trying the cold-turkey cure, and those candy bars had become a counter-fixation. Unfortunately the candy was gone already, used as food for the group. Karen had eaten more than her share. Distraction was best, now.

Zena brought out the battered cards. "Honeymoon bridge again?"

"Yes!" It was like grasping a liferaft.

But the game did not go well, though Karen was ordinarily a good hand at it. She misplayed frequently. "Can't you even see the cards?" Zena asked sharply. "You just threw away an ace from your dummy, dummy!"

"I thought it was a deuce."

"A deuce! You're seeing double!"

"More like a blur," Karen admitted.

"Karen, are you *sure* you don't want to say something?"

"What?"

"You're shaking, you're panting, you're cross-eyed. Are you ill?"

"I'm hungry! Some sugar. . . ."

"Forget the darn sugar!"

Gus looked back from the front seat. "You mean 'damn,' don't you?"

"Damn!" Zena cried with feeling. It *was* a better word. "Karen, I asked you a question!"

Karen looked confused. "What question?"

"Are you ill? Or is it—something else?"

"Something else?"

Zena threw her hands up in an overdramatic gesture that cost her half her cards. "You're evading the issue!"

"I wonder where it is?" Karen murmured, standing unsteadily.

"Where *what* is?"

"The issue." Karen leaned over to peer under the table. "Not here."

Zena, sure now that she was being mocked, was silent.

Karen tried to stand erect again, but lost her balance and spun sidewise, half-falling against the table. One hand struck the wall that enclosed the adjacent shower-stall. Zena was shocked to see blood welling from scraped knuckles. This had passed beyond the joking stage!

But Karen didn't seem to notice. "Got to go home," she said, trying again to stand.

"You can't go home! Look at your hand!"

She looked. "Oooo, icky! Must wash it. Take a shower." She started to undress.

They had undressed in semi-public many times, but this was different. No one was going out into the rain now. "Stop the bus!" Zena cried, alarmed. "Karen's sick!"

Thatch obligingly slowed the vehicle. Gloria appeared, in her nightgown and curlers. Zena noted that only passingly: hair curlers for a *wig*?

"Who are you, miss?" Karen demanded.

"You know Gloria," Zena said. "Gloria, Gordon, our cook?"

Karen whirled around, letting her shirt fling wide, and fell against Gloria. "Hello, Gloria Gordon! What kind of a lesbian are you?"

Gloria looked puzzled, but automatically caught her. The sight of Karen's genuine bosom against Gloria's false one disgusted Zena. "Are you feeling well?" Gloria asked.

"No," Karen said, and began to cry. "Zena's been teasing me."

"She's been getting worse—" Zena said, stung. "I think it's withdrawal."

"Sugar," Karen blubbered.

"Sugar," Gloria repeated. Then, abruptly: "God, yes! Get her some sugar, right away!"

Thatch shook his head. "We don't have any. She ate it all before."

"Well, something sweet!" Gloria cried. "Quick, it's an emergency!"

"This is no time for candy—" Zena began.

"Can't you see," Gloria said. "It's hypoglycemia."

"What?"

"Low blood sugar. Insulin shock. This girl has diabetes!"

"Diabetes!" Zena echoed, mouth open.

Thatch dived into the breadbox. "Here's an old sweet roll."

"Break off a piece with icing and put it in her mouth. Hurry—before she goes into shock!"

Thatch obeyed. Gingerly he pushed a fragment between Karen's teeth while Gloria held her upright. "Chew it, dear," Gloria said. "Swallow. Don't choke, now! That's it!"

Karen did so. They fed her another piece.

In less than a minute she straightened and looked around. "What am I doing here?" Karen asked. "Why are you holding me?"

"She *couldn't* recover that fast!" Zena said.

Gloria let Karen go, and made a warning motion to Zena. "You were about to pass out, dearie."

"Nonsense. I was playing cards with Zena." She paused. "Sugar."

"Why didn't you tell us you were diabetic?" Gloria demanded.

Karen sat down. "I see I banged my hand."

"Don't you remember?" Zena asked, still suspicious of these strange symptoms.

"That's right, I don't remember. I never do."

Thatch looked concerned. "How often does this happen?"

Karen took the rest of the sweet roll from his hand and began munching on it. "Only when I take insulin and then don't get enough to eat."

"Insulin is dangerous," Gloria said. "You could have gone right on into shock and died, because we didn't know. You should have told us!"

Karen looked at her. "Did you tell the folks about your condition—right off?"

Gloria's face froze. Then she smiled, a trifle grimly. Zena realized that shaving the chin must be a vital part of the Gordon-Gloria changeover, for any suggestion of a beard would have destroyed the effect. Gus and Thatch were getting to look like hoboes, but Gloria's cheek was smooth. "I see your point."

"*I* don't see it!" Gus said. "Changing clothes won't kill anyone. Going into a coma like this—"

"Not a coma," Karen said. "Shock. There's a difference."

"Different names for the same thing, aren't they?" Gus insisted. "You pass out—"

"With insulin shock I pass out because there is not enough glucose in my blood. With diabetic coma there is too *much*. Sugar wouldn't stop the coma."

"So you kept silent because you were embarrassed," Zena said.

"Not precisely," Karen said, licking the last crumbs off her fingers. "I realized from what you said that it would rain for a long time, and I didn't want to be stranded." She looked out the window, and the beat of rain seemed to become loud. "I have plenty of insulin, but without shelter or food—"

"What do you think we are!" Zena exclaimed.

"Practical people," Gloria answered for Karen. "Diabetics require more food, when they're on insulin—and they need it on schedule. She's a liability. Right, Gus?"

Zena was affronted. "How can you say a thing like that!"

"We can't put her out," Gus said, alarmed.

Then Zena realized Gloria's purpose. Gus was the one most likely to demand selection of the fittest—but he had already been subverted by Karen's sexual offerings. Gloria had challenged Gus and brought an automatic denial—and now it would be extremely difficult for Gus to reverse himself or to enforce an inhumane standard for the rest of them.

Unkind politics, but better than putting a sick woman out to die! No wonder Karen had been eager to be obliging. She had known that one day soon her life might depend on it.

"Get on with the driving, Thatch!" Gus said irritably.


On through the rain. Floy amused herself by trying to dance—and the result was pitiful. In the confines of the bus she only bruised herself against the furniture and made a racket. Sometimes Gordon danced with her, holding her very close so that she could not go astray—and that bothered Zena because she remembered Karen's 'lesbian' comment. Gordon was male, but viewed himself as female, and this body-flush-to-body motion with the awkward child—but of course she was inventing hobgoblins, Zena told herself. Floy would have driven them all crazy, if Gordon had not taken her in hand and found positive outlets for her graceless energies.

But what bothered Zena most was not external but internal—the subtleties of group interaction. Thatch drove, Gloria cooked, Floy and the cat stood guard at night, Gus exerted his peculiar type of leadership. Karen kept Gus happy. Every person was finding his function. Except Zena.

She tried to participate, but somehow found herself excluded. The foraging parties no longer included her, and there wasn't much to do inside the bus except play cards. She felt useless.

Not that the others held it against her. They were all oddly solicitous of her needs. She was not being shunted out of the party; rather she was being set up for some very special position obvious to everyone except *her*. What could it be?

They had reached high ground. The rain still came down, but there was no further concern about flooding. It would take weeks for the water to reach this height at an inch an hour.

"We'll have to get as far up in the mountains as we can," Gus said. "So we'll need a real load of supplies—grain, canned stuffs, medicine."

"It's all been raided," Thatch objected.

"Not by a long shot. Smart people are saving it. We just have to find their cache."

"Hey," Floy said, delighted. "We'll raid the raiders!"

"That's about it," Gus said grimly. "And they'll be tough cookies. But it's that or starve."

They kept watching for likely prospects. As they skirted a city—there was no way to tell which one it was, as all signs and landmarks had been altered by the storm—they saw lights at one large building. Only a temporary thinning of the attendant fog enabled them to see the glow from a distance. "Warehouse," Gus said with satisfaction. "Whatever they have in there, we need—you can bet on it."

"It'll be guarded," Thatch said. None of them bothered to raise moral objections any more; they had all long since recognized that the survival of the most competent was the new morality. "Guns, probably."

"And booby traps," Gordon said. "Otherwise it would have been raided and cleaned out by now."

"All of which makes it an excellent place to avoid," Zena said, growing alarmed.

"Which is what everyone else must have been thinking," Gus said. "By now they must be getting careless. Most of them sleeping, while only one or two guards are on duty.

Distract those, and we can take our pick of what's inside—so long as we make it fast."

"Fine, in theory," Gordon said. "But what's going to distract a couple of armed men looking out into the rain?"

"Girls, of course."

"Now wait a minute!" Zena said.

"Yes," Gordon agreed. "Nude or near-nude. Dancing, maybe. Striptease. That'd be good for five or ten minutes."

"I have no intention of—" Zena began, outraged.

Gus waved her aside. "Not you, of course. You'll guard the bus."

"What do you mean, 'of course'?" Zena demanded.

"I get the hint," Karen said. "He sees me as more the striptease type. Okay, if that's what it takes to put sugar on the table—"

"Not you either," Gus said. "You're needed at the other end."

"Surely you don't mean the child," Zena cried, proceeding from one sense of outrage to another.

"That child isn't badly built," Gus said. "Stand up, Floy."

Floy stood, putting her hand against the wall to prevent herself from lurching off balance. Gus put his hands about her waist, cinching it. "See, she's slim but female, and she's got a bust, too."

"Preposterous!" Zena cried.

"Can I dance?" Floy asked wistfully.

"That's the general idea, honey," Gus said.

"You know that won't work!" Zena said. "Gus, this is sickening!"

"She can dance," Gus said evenly. "She just needs the right music."

"Sure, that's right!" Floy said eagerly. "The music's always wrong! But *good* music—"

"This is pointlessly cruel!" Zena said.

"Will you shut up a minute?" Gus demanded. "Anything sexy is sickening or cruel to you! We've got a job to do."

Furious, Zena shut up. Better to find out exactly what Gus was up to, so that she could scotch it before someone got hurt.

"We don't have much in the way of musical instruments," Gus continued. "But we have some pans and tools. You'll have to play them yourselves, of course."

"Of course," Gordon agreed, taking up pan and screwdriver. He struck the one with the other, producing an unmusical clash. "You try it too, Floy."

Floy tried it too. Then they banged together, and the noise was earsplitting in the confines of the bus.

"Now dance," Gus said, holding his hands over his ears.

Floy flung out her arms. They smashed into the furniture. "Ow!" she yelled.

"Well, you need more room to do it right," Gus said. "That's been your problem all along. You have the idea, though."

"Do you really think it'll work?" Floy asked, so excited it was painful for Zena to watch.

"Sure!" Gus said. "So long as you give yourself room and beat the music right."

Gordon put on his blonde wig. "I hate to get this wet," he said.

"It's a good cause," Gus said. "Get back to the bathroom and convert. I'll talk to the others." Gordon went back, and Gus continued: "Now Thatch and Karen—you know what you have to do?"

They nodded. "But no killing," Karen said.

It was belatedly evident to Zena that much discussion and planning had been done while she was asleep. This whole thing had been blocked out in advance as a contingency, and now the pieces were meshing nicely.

Why had she been excluded? She was ready to help, to do her part; they all knew that. Every person in the group had to pull his weight for the survival of the whole.

Gloria came forward. "Now it has to be coordinated," Gus cautioned the rest. "We don't dare bring the bus too close at first, and when we do it'll be sans lights. If they don't go for the diversion, call it off immediately. We don't want to take losses."

"They'll go for the diversion," Gloria said. "You watch."

Zena felt numb. This was like a commando raid—and she was being excluded and ignored.

"Zena, sit up here," Gus said. "I think I have this driving straight, but you'll have to tell me if anything goes wrong.

Gus—driving? "I can drive it," she said.

"No, I know where it has to go," he said.

Zena shook her head with resignation and took the passenger's seat.

"Raiding party get out first," Gus said, fastening his hands tightly on the wheel. "We'll give you time to get close. Listen for the music."

"Check," Thatch said. "That's one thing about the rain—it'll cover our noise and our tracks."

Gus drove. It was clumsy, and the vehicle tended to wander, but he guided it down a side road toward the lighted building. Karen must have been instructing him, Zena realized. She could easily have told him about the basic rules of driving, and demonstrated, during those long shifts when the others were asleep or inattentive.

As the building loomed higher, Gus stopped, stalling the motor on the brake. "Now!"

Thatch and Karen got out and disappeared into the night. The rain closed in behind them like a wet shield. Gloria came up and helped Gus re-start the motor. "I'll walk ahead now," Gloria said. "You move along slowly without lights, and I'll whistle if I meet a hole or an obstruction."

"Right," Gus said. Zena saw that his hands were sweaty on the wheel. How had they prevailed on him to actually do useful work?

Slowly they proceeded. The darkness was not total; it

was possible to make out the general channel of the road between the buildings. Then the glowing torches of the building came into full view.

Gus turned off the motor and coasted. "Got to stop here. They might have a floodlight. Diversion squad—you circle around about halfway before you start. We don't want to lead them to the bus!"

"Right, dearie," Gloria said. "Floy, don't forget your music."

Floy picked up her pan and screwdriver and went out.

Zena abruptly realized that she was alone with Gus. Was *that* why she had been spared exterior duties? If so, she would toss him on his ear!

But he made no move toward her. His eyes were ahead, as he peered through the rain. "God, I hope this works!" he said.

"Why wasn't I included in?" Zena demanded, realizing that she was being perverse. She had been protesting when she thought she was going to be part of the "diversion."

"You *are* included in," he said. "It's important that you not risk yourself unnecessarily."

"While you send that child out to bang a pot and do a strip?"

"She enjoys it. It's what she can do."

"And what is it *I* can do?"

"Pipe down," he said. "It's about ready to start."

Zena clenched her teeth in a fury. This oaf was treating her like a child—and, worse, she was playing the role!

There was a faint banging, as of tools striking pans. And a kind of unmelodious singing.

Floodlights came on at the building. "They've got a generator!" Gus whispered. A spotlight played across the empty parking lot, searching for the sound. In a moment it picked out the two figures dancing in the rain.

Zena stared. From this distance, which was not as far as it seemed in the rain, Gloria looked just like a chorus girl and Floy looked like a woman. They were both gyrating in a manner that made Zena queasy inside, flinging their hips and chests about, and they were banging dissonantly on their instruments. First one flung aside a piece of apparel, then the other did. They really were doing a striptease!

The spotlight followed them as they wound closer to the building. Zena found their motions obscene. Gloria could not peel off much more without turning male, and little Floy—

Floy was dancing, really dancing! Her arms and legs were waving about matching the dubious music, and the jangle of the pans seemed to fit her style. She was dancing to the dissonance.

Zena could not take her eyes off that spectacle. She was appalled yet fascinated. There had never been free-form expression like this. Floy really did have a talent for it. The motions of her body were no longer uncoordinated; they reflected the beat of an unearthly music. The girl did have a woman's body, as Gus had noted—a body suddenly effective, in its inimitable fashion.

"I knew she could do it!" Gus murmured with satisfaction. It was as though he were a coach, watching his player perform on the field.

But he was right. He *had* told Floy she could do it— and now she could.

"Give me a piece like that any time!" Gus breathed.

"What?" Zena asked him sharply.

For the first time she saw him embarrassed. He had forgotten she was there. Yet she hardly felt she had scored any victory.

The spotlight moved away from the dancers. Then it clicked off entirely.

"Now!" Gus cried, exultant. "How the hell do I start this thing?"

Zena showed him how. They moved up to the front of the building.

Karen was just completing the tying and gagging of the

second man. "The other's inside," she called. "No booby traps, they claim. They know what'll happen if any of us get hurt. Keep an eye out to see reinforcements don't come."

"*What* will happen?" Zena asked, not expecting an answer. Obviously a threat had been made: an eye for an eye. She hoped it was a bluff—and she hoped the bluff worked.

It was a phenomenal haul. Food, clothing, medical supplies, books—they loaded the floor of the bus with as much as seemed safe to carry, then climbed aboard.

The last thing they did was to cut the bindings on their prisoners. "We haven't hurt you or your property," Gordon told the men. "All we've done is take what we need for survival. We won't be back. If you're smart, you won't go chasing after us—and next time you won't be taken in by any free shows! There's plenty of stuff left for you, and maybe this lesson will enable you to keep it longer."

Seeming dazed, the men showed no fight. There was no pursuit.


They found a suitable place with good elevation and good drainage, and camped there. The bus became a stationary home in the mountains. Gus and Karen moved into the back room permanently, while Gordon and Floy took the dropdown bed above the driving compartment. Zena slept in the dinette, while Thatch used the mattress from the rear ceiling bunk, now placed on the floor. The rugs of course were ruined, and constantly wet.

It had been two weeks since the rain started, and it had eased at times but never abated. For every hour it slacked off to half-an-inch an hour, there was another hour at two inches an hour.

Thatch and Gordon went out each day to forage, for they knew their raided supplies would not last indefinitely. Floy and her cat went out frequently to explore the immediate neighborhood, guarding against ugly surprises. Sometimes Zena saw Floy dancing, alone in the rain, flinging about that body with sensual abandon. Karen set about making things out of the material now at hand: blankets and ponchos for inside and outside work.

Gus turned on the radio and plowed slowly through the static, searching for news. There wasn't any.

"It's all anybody can do to survive," Zena said. "Let alone broadcast. No facilities, no power."

"Try shortwave," Karen suggested.

Thatch spread an aerial wire outside and Gus tried band after band. There was some talking, but it was in a foreign language. Then an English broadcast, faint but distinguishable: ". . . severe erosion. Estimated losses: fifty percent."

They clustered around the set, listening to the clipped British accent. "Liverpool: completely flooded. Estimated height of water at sea: thirty-five feet. Effective height inland: sixty feet. Estimated losses: sixty percent. Edinburgh: completely flooded. Estimated height of water—"

"Those losses are *people*!" Zena exclaimed, appalled. "The British isles are drowning!"

"So are we," Gus said. "Shut up."

One day, Zena thought, she was going to push him out into the rain!

They listened to the grim chronicle of losses: one coastal city after another wiped out by the terrible tide.

"No further word from the Continent," the voice continued. "Estimates based on prior statistics extrapolated for the past day's fall: Amsterdam losses ninety percent, Brussels seventy-five percent, Paris eighty percent, Berlin—"

"Paris has nine million people!" Gordon cried. "Seven and a half million dead?"

"I believe it," Karen said. "We saw what happens."

"It's not just the water level," Zena said. "The food shipments break down, the ocean brine intrudes—"

"Hush!" Gus cried. "America's on!"

". . . ninety percent."

"What city?" Zena cried. "I didn't hear the—"

"New York," Gordon said. "The Hudson River run-off—"

"Can't be much better inland," Karen said.

"If you don't want to listen, go outside!" Gus yelled.

But they already had the story. The rain was world-wide, and things were worse overseas than here. At least there were mountain ranges in America!

Something had gone out of their existence, however. Until now it had been possible to imagine a dry refuge somewhere else in the world. Now they all knew there was none.

Gus dug out his raided books and commenced reading mysteries. Zena, afraid that the confinement and boredom would drive her crazy, read *Heaven and Earth*.

"This makes no sense at all!" she expostulated to Gus. "This Annular Theory takes no note of, and makes no allowance for, the theory of drifting continents. Most of the things Isaac Vail seeks to account for can also be explained by continental drift. The pattern of ice ages—"

"You're forgetting two things," Gus said.

"*What* two things?"

"First, Mr. Vail died in 1912—long before the continents started drifting. So you can't hold that against—"

"The continents have been drifting for billions of years!"

"You know what I mean. Second, look at *that*." He gestured at the rain outside. "The canopy is here again. Does your continental drift explain *that*?"

"No, it doesn't have to. The rain is here for another reason."

"Uh-huh," he said smugly.

"Oh, go listen to your radio!" she said.

He did. Or tried to. The rain continued—but not the

98

shortwave broadcasts. Zena estimated that between eighty and ninety feet of rain had fallen—and the British news was off the air.

Zena fell out of bed. "What happened?" she cried.

Thatch sat up on his floor mattress, rubbing his eyes. Floy stuck her head in the door and yelled: "It stopped!"

Zena stared at the window. A few drops of water dribbled down it—but the steady beat of rain was gone. No wonder her sleep had been disturbed!

Gloria rolled out of the upper bunk. "It's the fortieth night after the fortieth day," she said. "The flood is over!"

Zena checked the calendar. "Ridiculous!" she said. But forty days had been marked off.

They dressed and went outside, even Gus. The surface of the road was still slick, where it wasn't pitted or washed out, but no water was being added from the sky. The effect was eerie.

They returned to the bus and had a sober breakast. "Is it really over?" Floy asked. "Are you all going home now?"

Home. Zena turned away.

"This is our home now," Gus said. "And there may be more rain. We'll have to be careful, very careful."

Yes, there would be more rain. Zena knew that what had just passed was only a minor squall compared to what was to come. But how could she tell them that?

Now the dawn was coming. They stood in a row outside and watched the first sunrise in over a month. It was spectacular, for the massive moisture in the atmosphere made the rays of the sun splay grandiosely.

"Other survivors will be abroad soon," Gus said. "And they'll be hungry and not too civilized. We'll have to survey the entire area and double our guard."

Zena groaned inwardly, but knew he was right—again.

This could be the most dangerous period for them, because they had good shelter and good food.

By full daylight, unconscionably bright, they saw that erosion was horrendous. Zena estimated that approximately a hundred feet of rain had fallen. It had scoured the landscape, ripping out trees and houses, undercutting the road itself. What remained was a steaming wasteland seemingly bare of life.

Thatch and Gordon cut walking staffs and set out on an area hike. Gus and Karen returned to the bus to sleep. That left Zena and Floy for the nearby explorations and guard duty.

"At least they let me out!" Zena said. "I haven't been allowed to do anything useful for weeks!"

"You're lucky," Floy said, leaning heavily on her pole so as not to fall.

"What's lucky about it? Everybody has to pull his weight, and I'm eager to pull mine."

Floy shrugged awkwardly.

"Now don't you do it too!" Zena cried. "I haven't raised an issue about it because there's been no privacy—but something's going on. What's the big secret?"

"You really don't know?"

"Of course I don't know."

"Well, Gus says there's going to be a lot more rain. Enough to drown the whole world, maybe."

"Gus is right, for all the wrong reasons. But—"

"So we'll have to make more people. Babies."

Zena sighed. "Gus has had the making of babies on his mind from the outset. The mechanics of it, anyway. He and Karen—"

Floy shook her head. "Karen wouldn't live through it. That's why she uses an IUD. And I'm too young, Gordon says. But you—"

"That's enough!"

"Sorry. You said you wanted to know."

100

Zena paused beside a plain of bare bedrock, scoured clean by the water. "I'm not having any baby!"

"You're the only one who can. So Gus said to take care of you, because if anything happened to make you sterile—"

"I said *enough!*"

Floy fell silent and stepped over some rubble, using her stick as judiciously as she could. Out in the open she handled herself better, because she had more room to correct for error. Dust Devil leaped atop a boulder and peered about, tail switching. He smelled something.

"This is ridiculous!" Zena said.

"You're always saying that."

"That's no refutation."

"I wish I could do it," Floy said. "Maybe in another year—"

"Whatever for?"

"I'm not much for doing things, but I could take care of a baby," Floy said. "I'd make a strap for it, or a basket or something, so I couldn't drop it, and I'd nurse it—"

"Nurse it!"

"There isn't any other way," Floy said. "No store-bought formula—and what's wrong with it, anyway?"

"Let's talk about something else."

"Sure," Floy said. "But why does it make you sick?"

Zena moved ahead, not answering. There was, really, no answer: she had been raised conservatively, and somewhere along the way had developed a strong aversion to the sordid aspects of life. Her devotion to meteorology and science had kept such matters safely distant—until the rain came.

That reminded her, deviously, of the stupidity of men. What had happened to those aboard the space station? Would there ever be a rescue mission for them, or would they suffocate when they ran out of air? They were above the rain—but the rain meant their doom, too. Poetic justice, but it was a vicious poem.

"No forage anywhere near here," Thatch announced. "This is all slope, washed out to bedrock. We have to move on." And Gordon nodded soberly.

"Where are we?" Gus asked, bringing out the map.

"Somewhere in the approaches to the southern Appalachian range," Gordon replied. "Northern Georgia, probably. Not that it makes much difference now."

"Sure it makes a difference! We must be somewhere near Atlanta."

"That's right. We skirted a huge city a day or so before we parked. I figured that was Atlanta. That's how I knew we were reaching safe high ground."

"Atlanta's big enough, all right. Should be a lot of supplies there."

"We've been through that!" Zena objected. "Cities are dangerous!"

"So is starving," Gus retorted.

"If we head on into the mountains," Gordon said, "we should strike the major pine forests. Those are built to take rain; most of those trees probably survived. And where there are trees, there is soil—and life."

"How about gasoline?" Gus asked.

Gordon spread his hands. "Do we want to travel much?"

"I don't mind your forest notion," Gus said. "In fact, I like it. But we'll camp there in a lot more style if we load up first on gas, and canned goods, and batteries and books and seed grains—"

"Seed grains?" Karen asked.

"Sure. We're going to be farmers. We have to start raising our own food, if we expect to live any length of time. There won't be any corner grocery store."

Gordon puffed out his cheeks in a soundless sigh. "You've thought it through!"

But something about that plan bothered Zena. She couldn't pin down the thought, except that it had no connection to her sundry other objections about their pro-

102

posed lifestyle. Maybe she was merely inventing nebulous disasters.

"I don't like going to the city any better than you do," Gus said. "But our last haul was well worth it. If we can do that again, we'll be set for a long time to come. And if we can grow a decent crop, and raise some animals, we can have a good supply for the next rain. I've got the long haul in mind."

"We could all wind up dead for the short haul, heading into a big city," Zena said.

But the nearby landscape was so bleak that there didn't seem to be much of a choice. True, they might find intact pine forest further north—but they couldn't eat pine needles.

They moved out cautiously. There was only one shovel, and that was needed for almost continuous road repair—or outright road building. Where the concrete and asphalt had resisted the ravages of the rain and run-off, the underlying foundation often had not, so that whole sections of highway bridged gorges. It was easier and certainly safer to drive over straight bedrock wherever feasible.

It took three days to reach the environs of the city. The Chattahoochee River had spread its boundaries enormously and excavated a canyon through the city—a swath of nothingness. Even now, with the rain stopped, a sizable run-off remained, and flooding was bad. Many buildings still stood, and Zena was curious to know what was inside them. Forty days without electricity, or fuel, or food . . .

"Look there!" Gus cried, pointing.

It was a complex of tremendous fuel storage tanks. "All the gas we'll ever need!" Floy said excitedly.

"If no one else thought of it before us," Zena said.

"And if that's refined gasoline," Gordon said.

"All right," Gus said, taking charge. "We'll strike at night, same as before, it may be guarded. If we can find a tap or something, maybe we can get what we need without anybody knowing the difference. But we'll plan a good getaway route, just in case."

At night they moved in as close as they dared with the bus, then parked and made a stealthy approach. Karen and Zena watched the tanks from a reasonable distance. Floy and the cat waited further back, and Gus of course was in the bus. They were to relay signals if anything went wrong.

The two women waited for what seemed an interminable time. There were sounds from various directions, but nothing significant. "Could be stray animals," Zena whispered, not reassured.

Then something flew through the air. It landed with a pop and burst into flame. The entire area was illuminated—and Thatch and Gordon were shown up plainly beside the nearest tank.

"Raise your hands," a man's voice shouted. "We've got a machine gun trained on you."

A machine gun! Zena moved toward the voice, which was only fifty feet ahead of her. She knew Karen would fade back to relay the news. Zena dared not run, as her shoes would make too much noise.

Thatch and Gordon raised their hands. Men came out of the shadows—three, four of them. "So you're looking for gasoline, eh?" one said. "That means you've got a working truck, maybe. Where is it?"

Counter-trap—and they had walked into it.

Neither Thatch nor Gordon answered.

"Well, we'll make you talk!" the man said grimly. Something glinted in his hand.

Zena threw herself on the shapes by the machine gun. She clubbed one man on the back of the neck with the side of her hand, then wheeled to face the other. "Hey!" he yelled. Then he was rolling on the pavement, stunned by the force of her throw.

"Let them go!" Zena called to the group near the tank.

But even as she spoke, both men nearby rose and came at her. "It's a girl!" one exclaimed.

Zena dived for the machine gun. She had had a briefing in firing such a weapon once, but that had been a long time ago. She would have to bluff it.

She turned the gun on its tripod to cover the two. "Get back!" she cried.

A scuffle broke out near the tank. She glanced there, and saw in the light of the flare that the four men were piling on the two. This was quickly getting out of hand.

She pulled the trigger. Her hand caught somehow in the mechanism, so that a fold of skin was pinched, but it fired! She whirled the massive thing around to cover the tank group, while the two near men dropped to the ground. She didn't think she had hit anyone; they were merely getting out of the way—as well they might!

"Someone's got the gun!" one of the nearby men yelled.

"Charge it!" one of the four by the tank yelled back. "We'll grab these two as hostages!"

Zena knew they would do it. In moments Thatch and Gordon would be captive and probably dead—and her, too. There could be no honor or mercy, after the devastation of the rain. She saw the men in motion.

She pulled the trigger and held it down. The machine gun vibrated as the bullets poured forth. She swept the muzzle through a wide arc, trying to avoid the area where Thatch and Gordon were. There was a scream.

A shape charged upon her. She spun the gun again and let go another burst. The man crashed down beside her, his body touching her elbow, and she knew he was dead or dying.

"Thatch! Thatch!" she cried. "Get out of there! I've got the gun!" She had the sick feeling that she had hit him too.

But a shape got up near the tank. "Right!" Thatch's voice came. He started to run.

Two more shapes lifted. "Which one's Gordon?" Zena screamed, not daring to fire.

"Gordon's gone already!" Thatch called back.

What did that mean? She saw the two figures converge on the one. The gun vibrated again. The two fell.

"Enough! Enough, Zena!" It was Gordon's voice, from close at hand.

But she couldn't stop. There was something about that massive, savage weapon with its shuddering death that infused power into her hands and arms and body, locking her grip. The stream of bullets continued to flow, pounding into the metal of the huge tank that acted as a backstop. There was the heady smell of gasoline.

"Stop!" Gordon cried. "You're holing the tank!" He dropped to his knees and yanked her hands away from the gun.

Too late. A sheet of fire rose from the region of the torch and engulfed the tank. Gasoline was leaking out and burning as it emerged.

"Back! Back!" Gordon cried, hauling her up.

They ran, raggedly. Zena stumbled and felt a pain shooting through her foot. But she had to go on, limping; the foot seemed able to bear weight.

Gordon hauled her around the corner of a building. "God, I hope Thatch gets clear!" he gasped.

Then the big tank ignited. There was a sort of whoosh and a flare of light. Zena had a picture of a human figure silhouetted against the blast. Thatch?

"Come *on!*" Gordon yelled, pulling at her arm. When she didn't move, he stopped and put his shoulder under her body and picked her up. He ran with her away from the ballooning heat and noise.

"Thatch! Thatch! Thatch!" she cried, over and over.

"I don't know! I don't know!" Gordon yelled back.

The terrible light faded somewhat as they put another building between it and them. Now they were near the bus.

Karen was there, and Floy. "I knew it wasn't safe to go near you and that machine gun," Karen explained. "So I brought word back about the trouble. Then we heard the tank go off—"

"Thatch! Thatch!" Zena cried as Gordon set her down. "Ow! My ankle!"

"He told me to move out while he covered the rear," Gordon said. "I thought he was right behind me."

"I must have shot him!" Zena said with a sick certainty.

"God Almighty!" Gus swore. "You shot Thatch?"

"I was trying to stop the men chasing him."

"She hit the tank," Gordon said. "That's why it went off."

Karen looked at Zena's hands. "This one's bleeding," she said.

"Forget that!" Gus shouted. "Get out and find Thatch!"

There was a second boom. Bright, roiling smoke rose over the buildings. "All those tanks are going to go!" Gordon said. "If he's near there, it's hopeless."

"You bitch!" Gus yelled at Zena. "It's your fault!"

Zena could not defend herself. It *was* her fault.

Dust Devil jumped from Floy's shoulder and bounded into the night. There was the sound of someone approaching.

"They've found us!" Karen cried, shrinking back. Normally she was unflappable; but her limit had been passed. Or she was running low on blood sugar again.

"No, that's him," Floy said. "Dust Devil doesn't run to anyone he doesn't know. Not like that."

It was him. "I had to be sure no one followed us," Thatch said. "I circled around."

"Let's go!" Gus cried. They piled into the bus, and Gordon drove it rapidly along their escape route.

No one spoke to Zena again. What could they say: that it was all right that she had messed up the whole project, set fire to the very gasoline they had come for, and almost shot Thatch?

# Chapter 5: Rape

"We have enough to get us back where we were," Gordon said. "After that, we're stationary."

"We'll be better off in the forest," Gus said glumly.

The trip that had taken three days down took only hours back, for they knew the route and had no further need for caution. Their laborious road-building paid off in need, in speed. But it also blazed a trail for the city men to follow, later.

They passed their prior stop and went on. The meter for the gasoline read empty, and the last of their reserve gallons was in the tank.

Now they had to slow, for they had no pieced-together road here, and wanted none. Gordon turned off the motor whenever they stopped for construction, and coasted wherever he could. Sometimes they used the pulleys, so that the bus could traverse seemingly impassable terrain with minimum disturbance. If they were lucky, it would fool the pursuit.

"Trees!" Floy cried happily.

The forest began—tightly meshed pine trees. Gordon pulled into the forest as far as possible, found a sheltered, level place, and stopped. "We made it!" he said. "And we still have a few drops left for an emergency."

Just in time, for it was dusk. They had spent all night and all day without noticing it, getting away from the city and into the high wilderness. Zena's hands were ingrained with dirt, and she had several painful blisters.

"Okay," Gus said. "We'll sleep here tonight and take stock in the morning. Floy stands guard until midnight, then Glory."

"I'll do it," Zena said. "Gordon needs some rest."

"Sure he does—but you can't do it!" Gus snapped. "You have a bad hand and foot and you've been working your ass off and you lose your head in a crisis. You've got to take care of yourself."

So that she could be a breeder, she thought bitterly. Gus didn't care about her welfare; he was thinking of posterity. He was taking care of her the same way he would a ten-gallon drum of gasoline: needed for future use.

Karen fixed supper and they all ate, sparingly. Then Floy went out with her cat, Gordon rolled into his bunk, and Gus took Karen to the back room.

Zena lay on her dinette-bed, wide awake. Why had she done it? How could she have blundered so? In retrospect it was obvious that she should have stopped firing the machine gun the moment the two men following Thatch went down. Instead she had hysterically blasted the tank and precipitated the conflagration.

She *had* lost her head. And she had murdered several men.

"Zena?" Thatch said from the floor.

"Oh, Thatch—I'm *sorry!*" she said miserably.

He sat up. "I just wanted to say—I thought we were

109

finished when those men ambushed us. They had knives, and they were going to use them to make us tell where the bus was. The idea of torture—it terrifies me. When you took over the machine gun—"

"I ruined everything!" she finished.

Gordon dropped down from his bed. "You saved our lives!" he said. "Nothing less would have made those bastards stop."

Pleased by this unexpected support, Zena did not know how to express herself. "You forgot to change!" she said. Always before it had been Gloria who slept.

"That whole project was ill-conceived," Gordon continued. "You were the only one who argued against it. We should have known there would be no more free gasoline. You did the right thing, breaking up the mousetrap." Then he looked at his wig, hanging on a hook by the bed. "I didn't forget. I took it off. I'm going out to take a walk with Floy." He went out.

Zena felt tears in her eyes. "He's generous," she said.

"Floy prefers him as a man," Thatch said.

"That isn't what I meant," she said, embarrassed. Was this Floy-Gordon thing becoming serious? A fourteen-year-old child. . . .

"He's right," Thatch said. "Gus was mad because his plan didn't work out. He doesn't like being wrong. We never had a chance."

"Oh, let it drop!"

"I thought I was going to die. You saved us. The sound of that gun was the sweetest thing I ever heard. And it was brilliant of you to hole the tank, so that they'd be too distracted to organize a pursuit."

"That was an accident!"

"Oh." There was an awkward pause. "Well, I just wanted to thank you."

Just like that, she thought. Thatch decided she had saved his life, so he gave her a formal, almost dispassionate thank-you. Because it was the proper thing to do.

"Nobody ever helped me like that before," he said. "Except Gus."

Except Gus. Zena felt a wave of nausea. There seemed to be no immediate cause. Certainly she did not object to weaning Thatch away from Gus. So what was bothering her now?

She thought it through, and realized that it was not the result of what had happened, but the anticipation of what was about to happen.

She got down beside Thatch on his mattress. "I can't do anything else right," she said. "And I'm not going to be much good at this. But I guess it's time."

"Zena, don't—"

"No, it has to be. I've proved I can't do anything else, as I said. I'll be stiff as a board and I may throw up, but Gus is right. It has to be."

"Zena, this is preposterous!" he said alarmed.

"That's my line, not yours."

"Without love, without joy—"

"Take it or leave it," she said, though she was trembling so violently she was sure he noticed. "Do you want me to go to Gordon instead?"

He pondered. "Maybe you'd better."

"What?"

"Or Gus. He always knows what to do."

"I ought to slap you!"

"Yes."

Her fear was replaced by a stunted kind of fury. "I don't understand you at all!"

"I don't know what to do," he said. "Going into something without knowing, without planning—that's asking for trouble."

"So I discovered, yesterday."

"I didn't mean that."

"Don't make me feel even worse."

"I'm trying not to. You're too nice a girl to—it wouldn't be right. I don't know what to do."

111

"You said that. Maybe you need to start with Karen."

"Yes. She's experienced. She offered—"

"She *did*!"

"She has to take a lot of food, so she said she wanted to make it up to us any way she could. She thought it would make things easier for you and Floy if she just handled everything in that line. Until things were more settled."

"She's probably right. But she doesn't dare have a baby."

"Yes."

"Did Gordon—?"

"No. He's ambiguous about sex."

"Why didn't you?"

"I suppose I should have."

"Thatch, you knew it had to come to this eventually. You can't turn down experience, then plead no experience."

"I think I'd know what to do if there were love."

*If there were love. . . .*

"You know, Thatch, when I came down here, I was afraid. But I see that I don't have to be."

"Yes."

"Will you stop saying 'yes'!"

"Sorry."

"Because you aren't like the men I have known. Or thought I knew. You really aren't going to push."

"I'm glad you understand. It wouldn't be right."

Once she would have accused him of homosexual inclinations, but now she knew that his relationship with Gus was not of that nature. The two men had their peculiar social and intellectual interdependence, but in other matters they were separate. Instead she tried another thrust: "Because there must be love, and you don't love me."

He was silent.

"Did I say something wrong?" she asked after a moment.

"No, of course not. There can't be love unless it's mutual."

She felt a thrill of something unfamiliar. "Are you saying you *do?*"

"No, no, no, I didn't say that. It isn't right."

She felt the sting of tears in her eyes again. "Thatch, you never said anything!"

"There was never anything to say."

"I can't love anyone. I don't know why."

"Maybe you never got to know anyone well enough."

"Did *you?*"

"Gus always handled things."

"Especially the girls!"

"Yes."

"Well, I can't stand Gus."

"Maybe you should get back on your bed now."

She took a breath. "No, I came here for a purpose."

"But I told you—"

"Couldn't you do it platonically? Weeks of group effort have gone into fattening this lamb for the slaughter! Mustn't waste it. You are the least of evils, you know." She was aware that she was making it about as inviting as an enema, but couldn't help her own perversity.

"No. Not platonically. Not with you. It would destroy—"

"Destroy what?" What was the answer she sought?

"Any chance for a real . . . ." He did not finish.

He wanted her love, not her body. He wanted too much.

"When a horse breaks a leg," she said, "you shoot him. Because it's better than letting him suffer. You don't have to love the horse."

"What has that to do with—"

She laughed, not easily. "I hurt my ankle." Did people still speak of a pregnant girl as one who had 'sprained her ankle'?

"It will get better."

113

"You're not much for analogy, are you?"

"No."

"It has to be done, and if I don't do it this time I'll never get up my nerve again. It would disgust me to have to get aggressive, and I might retch on you." She lifted her head to look at him. "Please, Thatch—I'll just lie here, and you do it. Quickly. I've gone as far as I can."

"I don't like this," he said, and she knew he meant it. She was not insulted, knowing his reason.

"I know it's not fair to you. I wish I could be like Karen. But I can't."

"If you were like Karen, I couldn't love—"

"So it has to be like an operation," she said quickly, refusing to hear what would embarrass her. Love was a gift that had to be returned. "And I hope it doesn't hurt too much."

"I would never want to hurt you."

She sat up and struggled out of her clothes. "I want to be hurt. I didn't realize it until just now, but I want to be punished. Because I fouled up the gasoline mission."

"Zena!" he said, sounding anguished.

She would have felt better if he had told her to shut up in gutter language. But of course that was not his way. Thatch always gave way to others, concealing his substantial talents even from himself. So he became less than he might be—and would not budge from that subservience.

She forced another laugh. Who was she to talk about being less than one might be! She had the figure and the health to put Karen to shame—but the very notion was sickening. "I'm making you out to be an instrument of torture, aren't I." She put her hand on his, and felt him shaking. "I take it all back. If I need punishment, it surely dates from decades ago. I have to get pregnant, so Gus will get off my back, and I'd rather it be yours. Maybe you could call that love."

"I wish it were," he said wistfully.

*I wish it were, too,* she thought—but could not say it. "You *do* know what to do, don't you?"

"Tell me to stop, if—"

She was taken aback. She had anticipated yet another demurral, and perhaps an extension of the debate until Gordon returned, at which point the affair would have to be cut off. Thus she would gain credit for trying—and failing through circumstances.

She called herself a hypocrite, and decided to go through with it no matter what. She spread her legs and pulled him against her. He was heavy, making breathing difficult. The position wasn't right, and he had to back off to adjust. *Maybe he'll give up!* she thought wildly.

But she had really given him a directive, and Thatch always followed through on directives, however unreasonable they might seem. There was a probing, and, oddly, excitement. She was crossing a long-feared boundary, going off the high board with the icy water far below . . . and suddenly there was pain.


She gasped for breath. Slowly, shallowly, it came. She realized that she had blacked out for an instant. She turned her head, feeling the weight of her eyeballs, and saw her surroundings.

She was in a space ship, breaking free of Earth's well of gravity. The lone civilian meteorologist to be consulted on this classified paramilitary project.

Somewhere there was pain. She squirmed, but could not alleviate it at the moment.

"You are conversant with the power crisis," the officer said to her. "With civilian mismanagement, fossil fuels banned, and nuclear equipment not yet sufficient, we have to have a cheap, nonpolluting, *now* source of power. Obviously, this is the sun. There is enough energy in a few square miles of sunlight over Earth to produce a million kilowatts of clean power. The problem is putting the mir-

115

rors into orbit. If we can find a way to focus that light without mirrors, we've got it licked."

"It will take more than a million kilowatts to fill Earth's power deficit," Zena said.

"We plan to set up the equivalent of a thousand million-kilowatt stations," he said. "In a band about the equator. This will be an adequate temporary relief to the energy shortage."

"Just like that? A billion kilowatts? With no mirrors?"

"No artificial mirrors. Actually, ice is a fine reflective surface. Picture what a ring of ice around the world would do."

"You would still have to get the ice there—and you could hardly take it from the oceans."

He showed her a slide. "This is a nebula," he said. "A small one, containing only a few billion tons of matter—ninety-five per cent of which is ice. It is drifting in a course that will miss Earth by only a few million miles."

"Suddenly I see. You want to divert this icy nebula to intersect exactly with the orbit of Earth. And use all that ice to set up a cloud of crystalline mirrors."

"Precisely. The ice will form a pattern of concentric circles about the Earth, each highly reflective. Stations on the ground will receive that focused light and process it into usable power. In less than a year the energy will be flowing—the cheapest source yet available—and the cleanest."

"Too simplistic," she said. "The mere presence of ice rings will not guarantee a usable focus of light. They would have to be precisely oriented. And the ice would soon melt, because Earth is much closer to the sun than Saturn is. And the energy required to divert the nebula even slightly—"

"Here are the calculations," he said with military smugness. "You will see that the orientation is, indeed, precise—an equatorial orbit angled to provide the necessary amount of reflection. There will be four rings, the outer ones shielding the inner ones from precipitous heat so that

116

they will not melt rapidly. The system does not have to be permanent; it is projected to last fifty years, during which period more durable sources of energy will be developed. And as for diverting the nebula—"

He paused with a satisfied smile. "Come this way."

He showed her a gravity-free chamber in the center of the station. "Observe the cloud of ice crystals on the left," he said. He pushed a button, and a jet of vapor shot out, making her feel inexplicably queasy. The water quickly crystallized, forming a cloud of frozen particles that drifted on toward the center of the chamber.

"Now observe the action of Substance J-2." A smaller jet came from the opposite side, but this did not crystallize. "Only a twentieth the volume of the ice, and far less than that in mass—but an interesting reaction."

Zena already knew better than to inquire into the chemical identity of "J-2." These people guarded their secrets jealously, with or without reason. An offshoot from sinister researches?

The J-2 cloud met the ice. The explosion that resulted was soundless, since the chamber was airless. Ice shot out in a hemisphere—and the main body of the ice cloud reversed course. "Explosive interaction," the man said. "The J-2 is almost completely destroyed, but the recoil shifts the direction of the remainder of the ice. This will work in deep space as readily as here, as it occurs in a vacuum. J-2 is cheap, as these things go; all we have to do is fire the proper quantity to intersect the nebula at the proper angle, and it will change that nebula's course."

"It needs more consideration," she said, though she was impressed. It appeared that they really could bring the nebula to Earth! "There are too many opportunities for error, and we don't know what effect such a series of rings would have on the climate of the planet."

"That's why we brought you in," he said. "The conservation lobbyists squawked like a bunch of chickens when they heard about this—we're running down the source of that information leak now—and demanded a reassessment. Well, we're reasonable. You have forty-eight hours to study the proposal before implementation."

"Two days!" she exclaimed. "I can't begin to appraise it in that time! It will take weeks on a computer to consider the meteorological impact—"

"Sorry—our computer's tied up. But we have plenty of paper and a pencil for you. You'll find everything's in order."

She felt another pain. "No, Thatch—of course it doesn't hurt," she said, wincing.

The figures did seem to be in order, on gross examination. But they were all military figures, provided by the organization that had worked out this grandiose plan. Therefore they were suspect.

"By the way," the officer said as the two days expired. "There has been a small modification. The original attitude of the rings was inefficient for reflectivity, so the orbits have been changed from equatorial to polar. That will put the rings broadside to the sun, as it were, instead of edgewise. That one small change will multiply the reflective power a hundredfold, with no increase in investment."

Zena was stricken. "But the heat! The rings will melt and disintegrate!"

"Oh, they'll break down faster than they otherwise would have—but even as little as a decade will provide more power than half a century the other way. It is well worth it, since our power crisis is *now*."

"But the water!" she cried. "What do you think will happen to it, once the rings melt?"

"It'll dissipate in space," he said nonchalantly. "Some will fall to the ground. What of it?"

"What *of* it! Have you any idea what that amount of water would do to the climate of the planet? It would be the second Deluge!"

"Let's not exaggerate," he said. "Now it is time to

118

watch the J-2 missiles being launched. This is a great moment for Earth!"

"You can't do it!" she cried. "This is a disaster! At least run the revised figures through your own computer and get a projection for the time of breakdown. If—"

The officer frowned. "I knew it was a mistake to let a flighty civilian in on this. Our computer is occupied with more important matters than a rehash of a minor variation in one project. Now are you going to watch the launch or aren't you?"

"The rape of Earth!" she cried. "You don't know what you're doing!" It was like a physical pain, a literal rape, making her writhe.

"I'm sorry," Thatch said. "I—I got carried away, I guess. Did I hurt you?"

Zena reoriented. "Oh, no, of course not, Thatch!" He *had* hurt her, but she knew she must never admit that. "I was remembering things."

"Were you—were you ever raped?" he asked, looking at her with concern.

*Not before this!* "Thatch! What a notion! Of course not."

"You screamed something about rape—"

The rape of the Earth. "No, that was figurative. I—never mind! I must have passed out, and dreamed. Reliving something that happened weeks ago. Nothing to do with you."

"You passed out?" He sounded disappointed.

What should she say now? "This experience—it was too much to assimilate all at once. My mind must have shied away. I'm sorry if it made it worse for you."

"No, you were very much alive! I thought—" He broke off.

She had a certain sympathy. He had thought she was writhing with the pangs of fulfillment, when actually she

119

was reliving the colossal blunder that had precipitated the deluge. What a blow to his fragile ego!

"You did the right thing," she told him. "Thank you."

"You're welcome," he said disconsolately.

Her stomach started to heave. She turned her face aside quickly—but it was a false alarm. It was laughter.


"So it *is* an annular system!" Gus exclaimed. "Just as Vail said."

"Close enough," Zena said. "I don't know whether there was ever a natural one, but we have an artificial one now."

"It's natural! All you did was divert the nebula to bring it near Earth. Everything else happened just the way Vail said. If there's one ice nebula, there must be others; if even one passed Earth, it would account for everything."

"Yes," she said, not having the energy to quarrel. She still hurt from the siege of the night before, and from her prior injuries and exertions.

"Except for one thing," Gus said. "You say this ring was in polar orbit, not equatorial. So it wouldn't act like Vail's rings, would it?"

"That's complex to ascertain. Certainly the polar ring is less durable—in fact, it broke down in days, not years. But what the exact pattern of rainfall would be—"

"In the Vail canopy, the rain falls mostly at the poles," Gus said. "At least it does at first. The sky opens up, there, in a kind of circular window, and the stars shine through. We had our rain right here—the canopy never really formed."

"We certainly did have rain right here!" Gloria said. She was cooking something appetizing from unappetizing scraps: her special talent, much appreciated by the group. Gordon, oddly, could not cook well at all.

"In the equatorial orbit the rings match the spin of the planet," Zena said. "The canopy matches, too. But with

120

this polar orbit, the breakup should be much less uniform. Worst at the equator, probably. Just one more consequence of the original blunder."

"When the military mind blunders," Gus said, "it doesn't do it small!"

Zena thought of the raid on the gasoline tanks that Gus himself had planned. The type of mind was much the same.

"But at least the rain is over," Floy said.

Zena shook her head. "It is not over. This was only the first ring, of four—and not the largest."

"Oh, no!" Floy wailed.

"How do you know?" Gus asked.

"I studied the figures. They planned on four rings, each in a different orbit. The first and smallest in the center, as it were; the others outside, protecting it and contributing their own reflectivity. The second one out was to have about six times the mass of the first, for example. Of course all that came to naught when they set up the polar orbit, because the energy of the sun struck broadside—"

"They didn't send all the rings at once?"

"No. One at a time. Spaced about two months apart."

"They couldn't!" Gus exclaimed. "The first one has broken down all civilization. No way to mount the technology two months after this!"

Zena shook her head. "Would it were so! They sent the batches of J-2 out at 48 hour intervals. They arranged it so that the first contributed less mass and more velocity, so it arrived faster. The others are larger and slower—but inevitable. They are all on their way right now."

"Maybe they goofed it up," Floy said hopefully.

"I doubt it," Zena said. "The military mind is much sharper on detail than consequence. They won't have many little mistakes to interfere with their big mistake."

"Four deluges!" Gus said, pushing his fists into the sides of his head. "That's like the four parts of the last ice age."

121

"Gunz, Mindel, Riss and Wurm," Zena agreed morosely.

"We've had Gunz," Floy said. "The others will be worse?"

"I'm afraid so."

"How much worse?" Gus asked. "You said six times as much—"

"I can't give an exact figure, because I don't know how much will be lost in space or remain in the atmosphere. I'd guess we've had no more than a twentieth of the total rainfall—perhaps less."

"One twentieth!" Gus cried.

"There won't be anything left!" Floy said.

"It's not that bad," Zena said. "There's lots of land above two thousand feet elevation. The western plains—"

"But who can live on scoured bedrock?"

"We'll worry about that when we get to it," Gus said. "Right now, we have to gear for survival of the next deluge."

"Mindel," Floy said.

"And the ones after that," Gus continued. "We have to grow food, trap meat, build shelter. High enough to be safe from rising water."

"The bus will do," Gordon said. "We can add to it, once we get it parked. But we'll need enough gas to drive it up into the mountains."

"Right. We'll have to survey for parked cars anywhere within miles, and siphon out their gas. If we find enough, we can use the bus to haul in other equipment before we camp. We can make it all right, if we just consider the problems and get organized. Now I'll appoint teams—"

Dust Devil, who had been exploring among the trees, hissed. "He's found something!" Floy said, running toward the cat. Zena shook her head. That grotesque awkwardness still embarrassed her. Floy was a good night guard—but what else could she do?

"Hey!" Floy cried. "It's a dog!"

"Kill it," Gus said. "We need the meat."

Zena wanted to protest, but knew he was right again. They could not afford to take in stray animals, and they did need the meat.

"A puppy," Floy said. "His folks must have ditched him. Somebody come pick him up."

Thatch went over. "Careful," he said. "He may be wild—or rabid."

Gloria looked thoughtful. "A puppy should be trainable."

Gus paused. "You're right. We have to anticipate trouble. A good guard dog could make the difference."

"Why are you always looking for trouble?" Zena demanded, irritated. "All survivors will have to work together."

"Maybe they will. But until they forget about that gastank raid of ours, we'd better work alone."

Zena hadn't thought of that, but now she realized that this was what had given her misgivings about the raid from the outset. The survivors of that raid would be out to kill. Contact of any kind would be hazardous.

"Would you rather kill the dog?" Gus demanded, misunderstanding her silence.

Zena nodded "no."


They found gasoline, in small amounts. They set up a ten-gallon reserve to get up the mountain, and used the rest to drive about, picking up whatever supplies they could find. Karen checked over a deserted drug store for insulin, and Thatch found several hundred pounds of seed grains in a farm shed, already sprouting. They got gardening tools and hauled dirt and fertilizer to a forest glade in the mountains, and Zena became chief farmer. She had no prior experience, but she was unlikely to hurt herself in the course of this activity.

"Party night!" Gus cried. "Look what I liberated!" He held up a bottle of Scotch whiskey.

"Throw it away," Zena said. "We have a world of problems without aggravating them."

"All work and no play," Gus retorted. "I say, eat, drink, and be merry, for tomorrow is another day."

"Gus, you cheated!" Karen chided him. "You're already stewed."

"Have some yourself." He brought out a bottle of sweet brandy.

"I have to watch it," Karen said dubiously. "If I take too many calories, or forget my insulin—"

"We'll remind you," Gus said. "And here's some for you, Glory."

Gloria accepted the bottle. "White cooking wine!" she exclaimed, delighted. She put it away in a cupboard for future use.

"This is ridiculous!" Zena cried. "With so many things we need, to waste effort on this—"

Gloria looked at her. "Gus is right. We're a group, we have serious problems ahead. We'll be better off if we learn to get along together, to understand each other well. We need to get sloshed together—one time, at least."

"Yeah," Floy agreed, eagerly inspecting the wares.

Zena threw up her hands. "I'm outvoted, as usual."

"Here," Gus said, handing her *crème de menthe*.

Zena shook her head in wonder. She had always been partial to that particular liqueur. Gus had uncanny perception about this sort of thing.

They drank. Zena's fears proved to be unfounded; no one imbibed to excess. Karen was quite careful, Floy took only sips of each type, Thatch made one small glass of brandy last an hour, and Gloria evidently had a connoisseur's taste in alcohol. "Gordon gets drunk on hard liquor; I'm more discriminating," she explained.

Gus himself drank heartily, but only grew more affable. It was contagious, and Zena soon found herself pleasantly high. The awfulness of past events became bearable. She realized that some of this would have helped her with Thatch. Well, before long she would brace him again, and this time try to hang on to her consciousness. Sex was not an evil.

It *wasn't?* She caught herself in that mental dialogue and marveled. Were her fundamental values changing? What was the distinction between a Necessary Evil and a Means to an End?

"Whatcha thinking of, brown eyes?" Gus asked her.

"Green eyes," she said. "It's my hair that's brown."

"Funny," he said. "You look brown. Or black. Eyes. I must be getting drunk."

"That's right," Karen said. "Floy's the one with black eyes."

"Yeah," Floy agreed, obviously enjoying her first licit alcohol. " 'Cause I hit myself in the face so often."

"Black-eyed or not, you're a cute one," Gus said grandly. "You did just great in that dance."

"Yeah," Floy agreed, flattered.

"I'd take you to bed in a moment—"

"Why don't we sing a song?" Zena suggested quickly.

"Hey, pretty little black-eyed Susie," Gus sang, slopping his drink as he gestured expansively. "Hey, pretty little black-eyed Susie! Hey, pretty little black-eyed Susie, hey!"

"Hey, I like that song!" Floy said.

"Watch it," Zena warned. "Some of the words—"

"Susie and the boys went huckleberry picking," Gus continued jovially. "Boys got drunk and Susie got a licking!"

Zena joined in the chorus: "Hey, pretty little black-eyed Susie!"

"Susie and the boys went whiskey brewing, Boys got drunk and Susie got a—"

"*Licking!*" Zena finished loudly, drowning him out. Karen choked on a mouthful of brandy, laughing.

Undismayed, Gus went through the chorus and started

the next verse. "Susie and the boys went corn shucking—"

This time everybody shouted *"Licking!"*

Then Gloria tried a home-made verse in her husky voice: "Zena and the boys went ice-ring planing, Boys fouled up and Earth got a raining!" And the song dissolved into mirth.


Next morning they started the garden. Thatch and Gordon had already made a plateau of rich earth and boxed it in as well as possible. Now Zena planted the seeds according to the instructions on each package.

"We'll need a privy," Gus said. "Nothing like human ordure to fertilize a garden; mustn't be wasted. I'll draw up the plans."

"And we'll need water," Zena said. "It may not rain for a long time. We'll have to haul it or pump it. A lot of it, if we want the plants to grow properly."

A fine beginning—but the weeds grew with far more vigor than the vegetables, and the insects were horrendous. Thatch and Gordon had to make a special foraging trip for weed killer and bug spray, for it wasn't only the garden that was attacked. Zena necessarily spent much time carefully pulling out each intruder without disturbing the tame plants. She didn't mind; it was peaceful and she felt useful.

Meanwhile, she saw much of the changing sky.

The second canopy was forming. Barely two weeks after the rains of Gunz ceased, Ring Mindel appeared—because it had taken six weeks for Gunz to form and rain itself out. This new ring was more massive, and higher in the sky. Day by day it spread across the heavens, twisting slowly about to form the equatorial attitude it should have had at the outset. That huge effort was costing it cohesion and stability, and so the ring that had been projected to endure fifty years would be in disarray in weeks. At that, its fate was better than that of the first ring, that had dissolved so precipitously that a formal canopy had never even formed.

At first Mindel was a thin vapor high in the heavens—two hundred miles, Zena thought. But it thickened and dropped lower, until the sun faded behind the mass of high cloud, and the under-surface of it was no further than a hundred miles above the ground.

Mindel was rotating. She could tell by irregularities in its structure, occasional rifts that let the sunlight through. It moved as fast as the sun, but opposite; a rift in it would rise in the west and set in the east twelve hours later.

But that was the least of it. The cloud cover was not even. It swirled in long strands, like a raveling rope or an endlessly writhing snake. Zena was fascinated by the slow undulations, seeing them as the struggles of an alien visitor: the ice nebula.

A reptile encircling the globe, like the Midgard Serpent of Norse myth. A creature whose poison overwhelmed the Earth in a great flood—as Mindel was about to do. How bad would that flood be? No one could really say; it depended on the efficiency of that misguided military project, intended to save the world by solving its power crisis simplistically—but actually destroying it.

Zena looked up, startled, a small weed in her hand. Midgard—Mindel. A coincidence of nomenclature, surely, but did it reflect reality? Götterdämmerung—the end of the world. The Biblical flood. Surely there *had* been a monstrous flood in antiquity; the mystery had been its cause. God had decreed it, perhaps, commanding the rain to fall, but no normal precipitation could actually have raised the level of the ocean. Could it have been such a canopy, visible as a snake or dragon in the sky, destined one day to swallow the entire Earth in the floods of its demise?

She stared at the massive, endless torso of Mindel, and began to believe. If man survived this, there would be new legends, similar to the old.

"There's a station!" Gus cried happily. "Someone's broadcasting again!"

"Ham," Gordon said. "Some ham got his equipment going again. Those hams are indomitable."

"I don't care who it is!" Gus said. "It's civilization!"

This turned out to be true and not true. The hams were now in operation—but their dialogue only confirmed the devastation wrought upon the world. Just over a hundred feet of rain had fallen, wiping out every major city the hams knew about. Now they spoke for small groups of survivors who were trying to organize a new nation built upon the highlands. Mechanics were putting motor vehicles back in operation; builders were constructing mass housing. The nearest reconstruction center was in Atlanta, though it was laboring under the handicap of senseless vandalism that had destroyed much of its fuel reserves. The radio invited anyone in the area to participate in the recivilization effort.

"They'd kill us," Gus said morosely. "We don't dare go near that place! Anywhere but there."

Thus they had forfeited their place in the new order. "It doesn't make much difference, really," Zena said. "There'll be more rain—lots more. It will wipe out everything they rebuild." She shared the guilt with Gus for that debacle: he for planning it, she for compounding it. Neither of them had anticipated the full cost of that endeavor, and both had to deprecate its importance. It did not make her like Gus any better, however; she was a partner with him in crime.

"If only we had *asked* them for what we needed," she groaned to herself. "Instead of coming as thieves."

# Chapter 6: Food

Dust Devil took to keeping Zena company in the garden, and the little cat was sociable enough in his way. He went after the larger insects—and these were becoming large indeed. Perhaps the presence of the puppy Foundling in the bus had encouraged the cat to seek other pastures, though the two animals seemed to tolerate each other well enough.

Usually Gordon hauled water for home and garden, carrying it in two buckets hung from a crude shoulder yoke. The best spring they had found was a mile away, so it was a time-consuming, tedious, tiring job. This time Karen came.

"Karen!" Zena cried. "You can't do that! You could go into shock!"

Karen carefully poured each bucket into the little irrigation trenches Zena had made, then came to sit by her.

"No danger of that. I regulate my insulin according to need—and hard exercise helps utilize the glucose in my system anyway." She sighed, looking at the meager rivulets her water had made. "But it is true I shouldn't overdo it. I'll rest for a while."

"Where's Gordon?"

"Out scouting with Thatch. This moss is growing over everything, making the terrain unfamiliar, so he has to be updated every so often." She shook her head. "I rather envy Gloria. When she gets tired or fed up, presto—a man!"

"Moss?"

"You're too absorbed in your garden, Zena! Haven't you noticed it?"

"I suppose I have. I just didn't realize its extent. I keep it out of the garden automatically."

They watched Dust Devil pounce on a huge brown beetle that had been bulldozing its way toward the garden. The thing buzzed and fought in a manner that made Zena shudder. If bugs now stood up to cats, what would be next?

"I think this cloud-cover encourages it," Karen said. "We don't get much direct sunlight any more."

"Yes. I hope we don't have trouble with vitamin D deficiency."

"Plenty of that in those vitamin pills we loaded up on. They'll last a year, at least—and the rain can't go on longer than that, can it?"

"Unlikely. Too bad we couldn't find you similar reserves of—" Zena paused, having second thoughts as she spoke, but it was too late. So she modified the subject and went on: "Would you mind explaining just what your insulin does? I know it keeps you going, but—"

"I could lecture for hours! But in essence, it's this way: I have what is called 'juvenile diabetes mellitus'. That's the most serious kind; for some reason children get it much worse than adults. It means a portion of my pancreas called the 'islets of Langerhans' that normally makes insulin has failed. Insulin is needed to get the glucose, the blood sugar, out of my blood and into my muscles. Without it, my body starves, no matter how much sugar piles up in my blood. It's like a trainload of food with nobody to unload it for the starving people. The pileup gets worse and worse—"

"That's why diabetics have sweet urine!" Zena exclaimed, understanding.

"That's why. So much sugar there that we're pissing it out—and dying for lack of it in our body cells. Real irony. So we take insulin, to make up for what our body lacks, and that does the job. But if we take too much, it uses up too much of the blood sugar, making a critical shortage, and—"

"Shock! I see it now. But you take more insulin when you're working hard—"

*"Less,* honey. Work helps the insulin, so I need less. If I don't cut down, I'm in trouble, unless I take more sugar."

"So you're really saving insulin when you do this water carrying."

"That's right. And since my supply is limited, that's all to the good."

Zena felt a sudden chill. She had gotten to like Karen as she understood her better; the woman was a hard worker with a steady temper. *"How* limited?"

"Don't worry! I use Lente U80—that's a fairly long-lasting combination, and strong. It doesn't need to be refrigerated. You've seen my hexagonal vials? Insulin is shape-coded. I have a good six months supply, and with careful management I can stretch it out—"

"Six months!" Zena cried, appalled. "What *then?"*

Karen looked at the sky. "Well, it doesn't keep forever, anyway. That's a pretty heaven."

"Karen—"

"But I don't understand that shape to the north. That set of cow horns. Is that the devil coming for us?"

How could Karen be so strong? It was death she contemplated in six months, or however long her insulin lasted. Certainly not more than a year. Yet she carried on without complaint.

Karen turned, concerned at Zena's silence. "Why Zena, you're crying," she said gently. "I'm sorry."

"I never cry!" Zena protested, wiping her face with the back of one dirty hand.

"Oh, you *should* cry! I cried a lot when this started—the needle, the sugar-watching. It's no shame."

"It is to me!"

"It shows you're human. No shame at all—so long as you get up afterwards and do what must be done. So that there is a continuity. I'm sure you will. Meanwhile I take it as a signal compliment—if your first tears are for me."

"Oh, Karen, this is awful! Can't we find some more insulin?"

"Only if some company still makes it. That's possible. Gus has been listening in on the radio, just in case."

Zena had thought Gus was merely entertaining himself instead of working. Now she was embarrassed. She had been misjudging people again.

"It is just possible that there is some in Atlanta . . ."

Atlanta. Where they dared not inquire.

"I really am curious about those horns," Karen reminded her. "I'm not unduly superstitious, but I feel watched."

Zena looked north. "It's the polar opening. The cloud canopy can't cover the globe entirely—there's nothing for it to rotate about at the poles. So it falls there, or fails to form, and leaves a circular opening. Nothing supernatural."

"But we can't see the north from here, and it's not a circle."

"The cloud layer is becoming reflective. The image bounces off the bottom surface and reaches us inverted. We only see part of it, and naturally it's distorted."

"You mean we're seeing around the horizon?"

"Two and a half thousand miles around," Zena said. "Maybe more. The effect will get stronger as the canopy thickens."

"Not the devil . . ."

"Not the devil!" They exchanged smiles.

The garden languished, but the sky grew in splendor. Halos of light appeared around the dimming sun—huge circular rainbows, with all their colors. At first they were hazy, extremely faint, but now they could be seen by anyone. Sometimes there was a double ring, and sometimes only a semicircle.

Still that serpent of Mindel writhed across the welkin, growing darker and stronger in its changing manifestations. Some days it hardly showed in the high haze; other days it seemed ready to swallow the sun itself.

Zena had a sobering thought: What if Mindel did not collapse before Riss arrived? Then the third ring of ice would overshadow the second canopy, and break down on top of it, forming either a double canopy or a doubly thick one. Which would make the eventual rain that much more severe.

And if that rain took longer than two months, as it probably would, considering how much water had to be cleared this time, the fourth ring, Wurm, would form on top of *that*. There would be not two, but three canopies breaking down together.

It would be one hell of a deluge.

Gus was trying the radio again, while Gloria washed the dishes. "Gus, I want to apologize," Zena said.

He glanced up. "Forget it."

"I haven't even told you what for!"

"It's about the radio, isn't it? I knew you'd understand when you thought it out."

"Have you found anything?"

"Lots of stuff. Nothing we can use. It would help if I could talk to them, ask questions."

"I understand there are five stages of dying," Gloria said.

"Nobody's going to die!" Gus snapped.

Gloria was unshaken. "The first is denial. The second is anger."

"How about *action?*" Gus growled.

"I'm thinking of inevitable death, that the patient knows is coming. Like leukemia, or—"

"Diabetes," Zena put in—and again was sorry. She spoke too often, now, before she thought.

"God won't let it happen," Gus said.

"God let the rings of ice happen!" Zena said.

"That's the third stage," Gloria said. "Bargaining with God. I'd respect prayer more if it came at occasions other than the last resort. The fourth stage is depression—and the last is acceptance."

"Karen has reached it," Zena said. "*I* haven't."

Gloria glanced at her. "You fight these things like a man. How would you like to exchange bodies with me?"

Gloria meant no offense, but the question floored Zena. Assume a male body? Her stomach knotted.

"Don't tease her, Glory," Gus said. "She's not transsexual, she's merely inhibited. Once she feels at ease, she'll be all woman."

"Thanks!" Zena said bitterly.

"That's the way it goes," Gus said. "First denial, then anger—and finally acceptance."

He was right about the anger, anyway.


Gus came out to look at the garden. "It isn't doing well," he said.

Zena's hand tightened on the hoe. "Give it a chance! It's only been two months since the rain stopped."

134

Gus carried a fistful of the little packages they had found in a garden store. "Carrots," he read off the first. "Ready in 78 days." He looked at Zena's row of carrots. "Are they going to be ready in 18 more days?"

Obviously they weren't. The tops were growing, but no significant carrot roots were forming.

"Lettuce," Gus read. "Ready in 45 days."

"We've been using it for a month," Zena said with a certain pride. "Also the chive."

"But none of it is going to seed," he pointed out. "What will we have for the next season?" He looked at another package. "Radish—ready in 23 days."

"I don't know what went wrong there. We got a few from the first planting, but these later ones don't seem to be developing. Maybe the soil—"

"Corn—12 weeks. Pumpkin—112 days. Cucumber—"

"What are you getting at?" Zena said irritably.

"I'm getting at the fact that there is a pattern to what isn't growing. We have not had a single plant form a root—a storage root—or go to seed. Not after Mindel spread its shadow across here."

Zena realized it was true. "Those first radishes were before that! The other plants—"

"That's right. Those plants need light to grow on—direct sunlight. Maybe ordinary clouds don't interfere too much, but Mindel is high and thick, with extraterrestrial impurities. The vegetables can grow, but the light trigger that makes them mature never comes. Maybe the soil affects it too; Gunz-water has soaked into it. But we aren't going to be able to do much more farming."

"We can eat the leaves," she said. "Carrot tops can be cooked, and turnip greens—"

Gus smiled. "Sure, Zena. I'm not deprecating your effort here. You've put in so many hours it's a wonder you're not stir-crazy. I just wanted you to understand that we can't live entirely on your garden, now or ever. Greens

135

won't keep; we need solid vegetables like potatoes, or grains, for storage. Or meat—plenty of it."

"We've pretty well cleaned out the edible wildlife we can catch around here," Zena said. "Foundling has a good nose and the hunting instinct."

"Except the bugs. I understand insects taste pretty good when you know how to fix them."

"Gus!"

"Yeah, it turns my stomach too! So we'll have to do what the others are doing, the way Thatch reports from his reconnoitering. Go fishing."

Floy emerged from the bus and came over. "Hey, I thought of something. I've been reading that Annular book."

"It's good reading," Gus said.

"It says people must have lived a long time, back when there was a canopy, thousands of years ago. Like in the Bible, maybe they really *did* live nine hundred years."

"Could be," Gus agreed. "The rays of the sun kill every living thing."

"But the sun is necessary to reproduction," Zena pointed out. "The plants—"

"That's what I was thinking," Floy said, perturbed. "If we need the sun to grow to maturity, will I be frozen like this, never quite big enough—"

"You're okay as you are," Gus said. "Don't let anybody tell you differently!"

But this time Floy was not put off by his compliment. "Never able to have a baby of my own? I don't care if I live nine hundred years, if I can't—"

"No babies!" Gus exclaimed. "God, I hadn't thought of that! We can't have a new order without—"

"We were talking about fishing," Zena said. "That's dangerous."

"Fishing? No more dangerous than starving," Gus said.

"The waters of the world have changed, Gus. There'll

136

be unpredictable currents, strange tides—and probably few fish."

"Should be plenty of fish!" he said. "All that water—"

"But it's fresh water! It will drive the salt fish away."

"Now where could they go?" he asked reasonably.

"Or kill them off in huge numbers. There could be disease—"

"Thatch says the fish exist. Maybe new species are taking the place of the old."

"It doesn't happen that rapidly! It would take them generations."

"Why don't we just go down to the shore and see?"

She sighed. Gus was usually right, even when he was wrong. A useful and obnoxious trait. "What do you want me to do?"

"And me!" Floy put in.

"Help make the net."

"The net?"

"The predator fishes come in close to land, Thatch says. Chasing the scavengers. The best way to catch them is by netting them. We may have to use the bus to haul the net out of the water, but we'll have plenty of food."

"It can't be that simple."

"It isn't. The word is those fish are fierce."

Zena laughed, and so did Floy. "Fierce fish!"

"The kind that survive in rough times," he said.


It took them a week to gather the line to make a strong net, and ten more days to fashion it. Gus insisted that every intersection be knotted precisely, and that every loop around the edge be tested. He had questioned Thatch closely and made many diagrams of his own, becoming expert in his fashion. Gus did not, however, do any of the finger-bruising work himself.

A question of a different and significant nature had developed in Zena's mind, meanwhile. By the time they

were ready for their first fishing expedition, she was sure,
But whom should she tell—and when?

They piled into the bus and drove down the mountain.
The ride was rough but strangely scenic. Zena had been
intent on her gardening and net-making, and had not
traveled since the ill-fated gasoline raid.

The forest was much as she had known it. But
abruptly at its edge the change began. She remembered
the desolation of bare rock, where the rain had washed
out every sign of human habitation or construction except
for sections of the highway and the most solid buildings.
Now it was all green.

The moss had sprouted everywhere, covering the
scoured surfaces and softening the bleak outlines. But this
did not improve the look of the land; it rendered it even
more foreign than before.

The steeper slopes, however, remained bare. In some
places there was a desert of packed sand with multicol-
ored rocks projecting jaggedly. Tufts of grass grew up
around the edges of the rock, and a number of tall weeds
had sprouted—but none of these had gone to seed.

Below, the land leveled out somewhat, and the vegetation became more lush. Still it was a matter of scattered
clusters of trees, a light covering of weeds, and the rest
filled in by the moss. There were no flowers. Small canyons
had been cut through what had once been rolling hills.

The shore, too, was strange. It was not the ocean, but
an arm of the Tennessee River, backed up behind the Appalachian range, maintained at super-flood stage by the
continuing runoff from the mountains. By the time it
dropped to more reasonable levels, Mindel's rain would
begin, and it would become a sea in fact as well as appearance.

Now dying trees projected from the placid water, and
there was no formal beach.

"First we have to cast the net, and get it out of sight

below the water," Gus said. "Let it sink right down to the bottom. Then we'll have to attract the fish."

"We can't spread it properly from the shore," Thatch said.

"Well, swim out with it. It has to be done right."

"It's not safe," Thatch said. "If there are large predators—"

"Of course it's not safe!" Gus said. "But they're not here yet. We'll have to lay it in a hurry."

But Thatch still balked at swimming far out, and Gordon agreed. "We'll have to make a boat," Gordon said.

They searched the shoreline for driftwood, and came up with assorted branches and trunks. They lashed this pile into a kind of raft. It looked clumsy and barely seaworthy, but it floated. Thatch lay on top of the pile and reached out and down with his hands to paddle on either side. Slowly he moved outward, trailing the net.

Fifty feet out he let the net sink, and started back. He floated higher now, for the net had been heavy. But his drift continued outward. "Oh-oh!" Gordon said. "There's a tow!"

Zena saw a flash of something farther out to sea. "They're coming!" she cried.

"We should have anticipated this!" Gordon exclaimed. "I'll carry out a rope. When I get there, pull us both in—fast!"

He dived into the water and stroked quickly toward the raft. But the fins of the approaching fish were faster. "They'll both get caught!" Zena cried.

Karen ran to the bus and brought out their rifles. She handed one to Zena. "Aim very carefully!" she cautioned.

Gordon reached the raft and scrambled on board. The thing shifted dizzily. "Pull!" he shouted. "Pull! Pull!"

Gus just stood there. Karen whirled around, the rifle leveled. "Pull that rope!" she screamed at Gus.

Startled, Gus began pulling. Karen aimed at the turbu-

139

lence in the water and waited. "For a moment I thought you were going to shoot Gus!" Zena said.

"For a moment I thought so too," Karen muttered. "We can't afford to sacrifice the only two real men we have!"

Thatch and Gordon were splashing madly to drive off the fish. Fins were circling completely around them now. Zena could make out the shapes in the water only dimly, but they looked inordinately large. And fast.

Then one leaped out of the water. Zena gasped. "What *is* it?"

"Shark, maybe," Karen said. "Or a sawfish. I don't know, but it must be a yard long. No trout, for sure! We're in trouble!"

Another jumped, and Karen's rifle went off. The fish splashed back into the water and immediately there was a vigorous disturbance there. "You hit it!" Zena cried.

"Oh, yes, I've used a rifle before," Karen said, preoccupied. "I doubt we can kill those things with bullets, but the blood makes them kill each other. Whatever you do, don't hit the men!"

Zena was in little danger of doing that. The image of men falling before her machine gun was before her, and of flaming gasoline, and the acute physical pain of first intercourse came again—her punishment for those killings. She did not dare fire!

Then another giant fish sailed out of the water toward the raft, and her rifle went off.

"Too high!" Karen said. "Bring your aim down."

"Porpoises!" Zena exclaimed. "Some of those are porpoises! Friends of man!"

"Not any more," Karen said. "Maybe when man was dominant, they were friends." Her rifle fired again. "But these are too small! Could they be giant piranhas?"

"How could a whole new species evolve in just a few months?"

"If there were canopy conditions before, canopy species

140

could have evolved then," Karen said. "Variants of the ones we know now. With the canopy back, they might metamorphose, returning to that prior state."

"I doubt it," Zena said. But she knew that animal life was capable of many unexplained phenomena—and there were the strange, vicious fish before her.

Now Gus had succeeded in hauling the raft into shallow water. It snagged on the bottom and began to fall apart. The two men jumped off and waded ashore. "The teeth on those things!" Gordon said.

"The net! The net!" Gus shouted.

They all rushed to their stations, hauling on the lines in unison. The net came up and forward, trapping the fish. The weight seemed to be enormous.

"Look at that!" Gordon cried.

Zena glanced at him, thinking he had seen a sea monster in the net; but he was staring at the sky. She followed his gaze, and froze in place.

A terrific band of color was there, like a rainbow, but almost a complete circle. In fact it was a double circle around the sun except that the sun itself could not be seen. Instead there were two or even four imitation suns intersected by the rings, each with a fiery comet-tail pointing outward. Faint rainbows were tangent to the outer ring, two below and one above. This brilliant complex filled the sky to the west, hanging above the water, making the cloud canopy seem suddenly darker.

Gus let go the net and dropped to his knees. "The end of the world!" he cried.

"Hold that net," Karen cried. But it was too late; the net had sunk, and the strange fish were escaping over the rim to free water.

"A sign from God!" Gus said, still staring.

"It's a prismatic effect of Mindel!" Gordon said. "You ought to know, it's in your book. A complex canopy halo formed by refraction through the cloud layer."

"But never like this!" Gus said.

"Riss just arrived," Zena said. "Two canopies joined together, intensifying the effect. Dramatically."

Slowly Gus came out of it. "I—suppose it is. I didn't know it would be like this, so bright, so big."

"Meanwhile we have lost our catch," Zena said ungraciously.

"We'll try it again tomorrow," Karen said. "We do have the dead fish—what's left of them."

"We'll camp here tonight and try first thing in the morning," Gordon said. He scooped out a piece of fish. "Not much here for us. I'm no naturalist, but these specimens seem quite strange. They must be freshwater species, but not the conventional game fish. I wonder—Loch Ness—"

"What are you talking about?" Gus demanded. "Loch Ness is in Scotland."

"The Loch Ness monster. There have been stories about many such creatures in isolated lakes of the world—that may not be so isolated any more. If conditions have been changed to favor them over the conventional species—"

"That's what *I* was saying!" Karen said. "And if that's so, we're in for an age of monsters like never before!"

"But these are *fish*," Gus said.

"Strange ones," Karen reminded him. "Who knows where they've been hiding, waiting for this day, this season?"

Zena watched the image in the sky, now fading. "It *is* rather like a sign," she said.

Karen looked at her. "You mean something by that, girl. Is it what I think you mean?"

"I suppose it is."

"Great news! We'll have a party!"

"Is it?" Zena asked. "Great news?"

But Karen was already telling the others. "Zena's got her baby! She's pregnant!"

Zena didn't have the nerve to look at Thatch to see how he was taking it. "Without marriage, without love," she

142

murmured, feeling let down now that the news was out. "How can it be good news?"

But the others were far more positive. Zena expected Gus to say "I didn't know you had it in you!" but she was spared that. "It *was* a sign of God!" Gus said. "That the plants may not procreate, but man will continue!"

"Not necessarily," Zena said. "This dates from before the Mindel canopy."

That surprised and dismayed Gus. Apparently it hadn't occurred to him that Zena could have engaged in such activity that early. It was satisfying to have kept the secret from him, and proof that Thatch did not engage in locker-room talk. But if it had not been for the gasoline-raid fiasco, Gus would have been right.

They did have a little party, breaking out the last bottle of cheap wine in their supply. They sang songs of the old world, the world of four months ago. The night was warm and bright, for Mindel now brought light around the globe, as though to make up for what it subtracted from the daytime. And Zena felt a little better.


Canopy Mindel/Riss loomed dark and low, so thick that daylight had become dusk and even the haloes had faded. Zena harvested the last of the chive and checked the ground in case she had missed any of the small turnips. Soon, now, Mindel would let go, and all vestige of the little garden would be washed out forever.

She heard a hammering back at the camp. Alarmed, she hurried back; Thatch and Gordon were out in the bus on a final foraging mission, not home yet.

It was Gus, using the sledgehammer to pound in a row of stakes. Zena stopped short and stared. Gus—working on his own?

"Come on," he yelled, seeing her. "Help me get these in."

"But why?" she asked, setting down her burden.

143

"I saw strangers scouting us. They know Mindel's going to let go soon. They want the bus."

"So you're building a palisade?"

"For defense. I figure they'll strike as the rain starts. I only hope it holds off until we get the bus in and the wall finished."

"I haven't seen any strangers."

"That's because you were working, not watching. They're there, all right—and they have guns."

Zena felt a chill. Gus had been right too many times before. He was lazy, but he didn't make many mistakes. That was how he earned his keep. If he took this threat seriously enough to do physical labor himself, she had better help!

But it took a great many stakes to make even a short wall, and Gus had not had time to prepare enough. Zena used the saw to lop off hard pine branches, and a hatchet to make points on the stakes already standing. It was awkward, fatiguing work.

Floy appeared with cat. "Hey, there's men around here," she said. "Dust Devil spotted them. I don't know what they're up to, but I don't like it."

"Then haul wood!" Gus said. "All our firewood has to be inside this stockade before the bus gets here."

They were still hard at work when the bus arrived. "Didn't like the look of Mindel," Gordon said as they pulled up. "We'd better buckle up for the deluge."

Foundling bounded out the door, a healthy and aggressive dog. His hackles rose as he sniffed the air. "He knows something," Gordon said, "and it's not the dragon in the sky he smells! Has anyone been snooping around here?"

"Yes," Floy said. "Dust Devil saw—"

"I think we'd better gird for an attack," Gordon said. "Nobody's bothered us before, but many people know we're here and the bus is a nice residence—particularly when it gets wet out. And someone may envy our women, too."

"Everybody carry a weapon," Gus said. "And stay inside the palisade. Don't give them a clear shot."

They had three firearms. Karen carried the pistol, while Gus and Thatch had the rifles. Zena and Gordon wore knives. Nervously they went about their preparations, completing the palisade and covering their firewood and other stores.

Nothing happened. Mindel hung on to its massive mists, and no attack came. Night advanced, darker than before; but the monstrous serpent writhed in the sky, bearing its own illumination. The guard was set, watching the eerie quiet. Zena slept nervously, one hand on her abdomen where the new life was forming, the other on the hilt of the knife.

In the morning Thatch made a small fire so that they could roast morsels of wild cow, conserving fuel for the bus's range. The odors drifted all over the neighborhood, but no strangers came forth. Still Dust Devil stalked about, hissing at nothing, and Foundling growled.

"I'm about ready to go and get them," Gordon muttered.

"That's what they want!" Gus said. "We'll stay right here." Then he looked at Gordon, considering. "Maybe you'd better change."

Gordon smiled grimly. "Yes. In case they come in peace."

He converted to Gloria, as fetchingly female as ever. There was no sign of knife or hatpin, but Zena knew they were handy. She remembered how shocking Gordon's first revelation of transsexuality had seemed—and thought of the contrast now. Gordon/Gloria had been accepted by this group for what he/she was, and that was important. Had this person ever before had such acceptance?

Could a female psyche actually have a male body? Dimly she remembered some clinical comment on the subject in a technical journal. Apparently it was possible. More likely the basis was psychological, but in any event,

145

Gordon believed it. He might in time have undertaken surgery for feminization, had the rains not come.

Now he would have to be a man. Floy needed him as such.

The day continued, and Mindel held off, taunting them with its potential devastation.

"We'd better sleep in the daytime," Gus decided. "Karen and I'll watch now, and the rest of you—" he paused, looking at his hand. "Wet," he said, surprised.

"It's started," Floy cried. "Mindel's first drop!" She clapped her hands as well as she could.

"One drop doth not a deluge make," Zena muttered. She did not enjoy the prospect of being cooped up in the bus for more months, short of food, and her baby coming.

But other drops were falling, making a patter across the dry ground.

Foundling growled, louder. "Oh-oh," Gus said. "Battle stations!"

Thatch took his rifle and crawled under the canvas covering the wood. Gloria donned a rain cape and stood in the bus door. The others stayed inside the vehicle, peering out the windows.

A man strode up to the palisade gate, solid and unshaven. "Starting to rain," he called. "Can I take shelter here?"

Zena tried to see him more clearly, but couldn't. There were several colonies of people in the neighborhood, but the voice was not familiar.

Gloria pushed open the door. "Sorry, mister," she said sweetly. "I don't feel quite safe letting strangers in."

The man paused, evidently taking her measure through the line of stakes. Gloria's measure, to the uninitiated, was impressive. "Well, can you give me directions how to reach the town? I'm lost."

"Of course," Gloria called. "Follow the tracks down to the coast, and turn left. There's a settlement about two miles along."

146

"I can't hear you," the man said.

Gloria stepped down delicately and moved through the increasing rain to the gate. "Follow the tracks, there behind you, down to the—"

"And could you give me a little water? Or a cup to catch this rain in?"

Gloria trekked back to the bus, took a cup, and brought it to the man. She had to open the gate to pass it through without spilling.

The man crashed against the gate, knocking her back. A pistol appeared in his hand. "Okay, men," he shouted.

Gloria's arm circled his throat, her knife glinting close. "Drop the gun," she said.

Instead the man whirled, thinking to throw the weak woman aside. The blade slashed across his throat, and he fell soundlessly.

Gloria jumped to bar the gate, but another man was already coming through. Gloria's shoulder hit him low, and he did a flip into the compound. Zena wanted to run out and help in the defense, but knew that would be suicidal. They did not know how many men the attacking party had.

Now three more men charged through the gate. "Fire!" Gus yelled. But he was the only one in a position to do so; Karen had to guard the rear approach. Gus did shoot, and one man cried out.

Then Thatch opened up from the woodpile. He fired three times, and two men went down. But Zena saw two more men rising over the rear of the palisade; evidently they had piled boxes or brush there during the distraction, and now could hurdle it. "Karen!"

Karen fired. One of the attackers cried out and fell back; the other came on over and landed near Thatch. A struggle ensued. Zena knew why Karen held her fire; she didn't know which man she might hit.

The rain was coming down heavily now. It beat upon

147

the metal roof and made a spray throughout the battle area.

A man lurched through the bus door. There was a livid scar across his cheek. Gloria must have slashed him in passing, Zena thought. No—it was not that recent. "Okay, girls," he yelled. "Up with your hands and off with your skirts!"

Zena made an underarm toss. Her knife flew at the man's face—but missed. So she charged him.

He was tough. She was unable to throw him in this confined space, and knew that in a moment his muscle would overcome her. Then something furry landed on his face, and he screamed.

Zena disengaged and found Floy there, her fingers curved and bearing nails like claws. Zena remembered the eyeball the cat had eaten before. "No!" she cried.

But the intruder had had enough. He half scrambled, half rolled down the steps and outside, where he found his feet and staggered off into the rain. Now Foundling's growling was audible; the dog was fighting too.

Suddenly all was quiet. Zena could not let herself believe that the attack was over, but a minute passed with no sound except the intensifying beat of rain.

"I'll check," Floy whispered. She went out, while Gus and Karen continued to watch at the windows. They had been right not to desert their posts; attackers could have come from any direction.

This time Floy screamed. "No!"

Zena scooped up her knife and leaped to the ground.

Bodies were lying there and the water that coursed away from them was pink. Floy huddled over one. It was Gordon, his wig knocked askew, his clothing ripped and stained red. To one side lay the man with his throat cut; to the other was someone with a monstrous hatpin protruding from his ear. Gordon himself had taken a bullet in the stomach.

Thatch appeared with his rifle. He was holding his left

148

arm crookedly, and blood dripped with the water. "Oh, God, did I do that?" he asked. "Did I shoot Gordon?"

Zena knew exactly how he felt.

Gordon opened his eyes. The rain splattered off his upturned face. "You idiot," he said. "Anyone can see it's a pistol wound." Actually his injury was concealed by the clothing, and Zena doubted it would be possible for any of them to tell what type of weapon had done it.

"Get him inside!" Floy shrieked.

"Don't bother," Gordon said. "Watch the perimeter." He closed his eyes for a moment, breathing in gasps. "Zena—"

"Yes," Zena said immediately. She was trying to get the cloth away from his wound, but already was certain it was an ugly one. "We have some morphine—"

"Meat," he said. "You have to have it. Use my body first, so that it doesn't spoil." He writhed, and caught his breath again. "Promise."

Zena looked at him with horror, and knew that he was dying. "Promise!" she said.

"Floy—your hand," he whispered. Floy took his hand with both of hers, her face wide-eyed and frozen. "I could have been a man with you. . . ."

"I know, I know!" Floy cried, leaning over him. "Oh please, please—"

Gordon shuddered again, then lay still. His eyes were open despite the rain. Alarmed, Zena felt for his pulse, but already she could see that he had stopped breathing.

Zena stood, and saw Thatch there. "I'd better check outside the gate," he said. "If they attack again—"

"Foundling will warn us," Zena said. "You come inside." She knew they had to leave Floy alone for a while. "How bad are you wounded?"

"Forearm," he said, letting her guide him. "Hurts, but not serious."

This turned out to be an accurate assessment. It was a wide grazing wound, bloody but not deep. Zena fixed a

149

tight compress and a sling, and he was able to function well enough.

They kept watch for fifteen minutes, but there was no further violence. Foundling scouted the area and came back, satisfied. They had driven off the attackers, killing four.

Floy hauled herself into the bus. "Shovel," she said grimly.

"We can't do it," Zena said. "We promised."

"I heard," Floy said, her voice level and empty. "But we have to bury something. And have a service. And a marker."

"His head," Karen said. "With the wig on it."

"No. He was a man. I want the wig."

The enormity of what they contemplated began to grow on Zena. "This—we can't actually—"

"I heard," Floy repeated. "I heard what he wanted. It has to be."

*It has to be.* The words struck at Zena, reminding her deviously of the new life inside her. Now there was a parallel emptiness in her, for Gordon had in many ways been the nicest and most effective member of the group. His sudden death was a double shock, because it was not the death she had girded for.

"I'll do it," Karen said.

And Karen was the second nicest. Even when niceness included the guts to do something utterly gruesome—for the common good.

They waited until morning, then set about the disposition of Gordon. "I don't know if I'm strong enough to get through it all myself," Karen said. "I'll use the knife if someone will hold."

Gus turned away, looking as sick as Zena felt. Floy sat in the driver's seat, the blonde wig on her head. Zena knew that she, Zena, should volunteer, but the job was too awful.

"I'll hold," Thatch said.

"You can't, with one arm!" Zena protested, though she felt relief.

"I must."

The two went out. Zena exchanged glances with Gus, knowing how he felt. They had known that there could be deaths in the group, but now that it had come there seemed to be no adequate means to handle it, emotionally. Except to go on, as Karen had said, taking care of the gruesome practical matters as necessary.

Gus took a rifle and stationed himself by his window, which faced away from the scene of activity. Zena went to the back and watched there. She had to trust that Floy would catch anything at the front. There could be another attack.

They waited silently for a long time, listening to the awful beat of Mindel's rain. It seemed as though the very world were being blasted away by this fall of water, much harsher than the first rain. Zena tried not to picture what Karen and Thatch were doing out there, but inchoate yet horrible pictures formed. Now and then she thought she heard an exclamation.

At last Thatch appeared in the doorway. He had a dripping package under his good arm. "Floy," he said.

Floy moved. She still wore the wig, which added to Zena's discomfort. "Now the shovel," she said dully.

"I'll do it!" Zena cried, wanting to participate in some way, hoping it would ameliorate the mixed distaste and guilt she felt. She took the shovel and went out around the bus. The rain soaked her in seconds, but it was as though her flesh were the metal of the vehicle, holding the wetness out from her personal core. All the bodies were covered by canvas now, fortunately.

Floy was behind her, clutching the package tightly. "I can feel his nose," she said.

Zena thought for a moment she was going to faint. She put her hand against the wall of the bus, steadying herself while her head cleared. "Where—"

"Anywhere," Floy said. "It's the thought that counts. He knows I love him."

Love. What a void this child spoke of!

Zena put her foot to the shovel and dug into the mud. The thought stayed with her, naggingly: Floy could speak of dismemberment and love at the same time, and mean it. Mean both. Zena could not comprehend either concept, herself. What was she made of?

"Sugar and spice," she muttered, scooping out the muck. How could they bury anything here?

"I don't know what I'll do without him," Floy said. "He was teaching me to dance."

Zena continued excavating. Who was she to give advice?

It seemed to take a long time, because the mud kept washing back into the hole. Thatch appeared, carrying a stone. "I tried to carve his name," he said. "Gordon Black. But it's all scratches."

"It will do," Floy said.

"I can't get it any deeper," Zena said, panting from her exertion. She tired easily, with the baby in her. "The water—"

"It will do." Slowly Floy unwrapped the package. Now, oddly, her hands were sure. In a moment Gordon's face was open to view, the eyes still open.

Solemnly Floy kissed it.

Then she re-wrapped it and set the bundle into the pool of dirty water in the hole. Now, at last, she stumbled, and had to catch her balance by dunking the head under the murky liquid. "Goodbye, Gordon," she said.

Thatch bowed his head, and Zena followed his example. "Rest in peace," he said. "We thought a lot of you."

"Amen," Zena said. Then she scraped mud in to cover it.

When the hole was full, Thatch set his scratched rock on top. It sank somewhat but stayed in place.

Floy turned to Zena. There was such childish woe in

her face that Zena dropped the shovel and put her arms about the girl. Wordlessly they stood there, both crying.

Mindel beat upon their backs, seeming now to be an extension of their tears.

# Chapter 7: Mindel

Thatch somehow managed to fashion a tepee out of canvas, with a flap on top designed to let smoke out while shielding the interior from rain. This was not entirely successful—nothing could really balk Mindel—but sufficed for the purpose. He made a fire inside. Karen went there, and in due course there was the aroma of roasting meat. It went on a long time, for there were five carcasses to process.

Zena was nauseated, but the two animals were stimulated by the fumes. Dust Devil stopped at the door, not liking the rain; Foundling hesitated, then went on out. In a moment the cat followed. They did not return immediately, so Zena knew they had been fed ... something.

The human party had meat for supper. No one was able to take more than a bite, but each person did that much. They had promised, and it had to be. Zena knew

154

the same word was going through all their minds, though it was unvoiced: cannibal.

Next morning Thatch strapped on a pistol—they had plenty of firearms now, because of the spoils of the battle—and took Foundling along for a survey of the region. "Be careful," Zena told him needlessly.

He was back in an hour. "They're gone," he said. "I found their camp, deserted."

The days went by. They scorched as much meat as possible so that it would nct spoil, but mold quickly sprouted on it. In fact, mold grew everywhere. It seemed to have gotten its start during the Gunz rain, and bided its time until Mindel gave it the solidly wet atmosphere it needed. Karen wiped it off the furniture every day.

Thatch's wound healed. He never made anything of it, though Zena was sure it hurt him. This silent suffering was not a thing she understood. Most people would have used such an injury as a pretext to rest a few days, at least, but Thatch neither expected nor desired such treatment.

One person was always assigned to guard duty, which meant marching around the palisade, getting wet. No raincoat or poncho sufficed in that downpour, and soon they changed tactics. Anyone going outside went naked. The rain was warm, not cold; the hothouse effect had heated it. Zena was not eager to doff her clothes, particularly since her abdomen was beginning to round out, but she was spared that. The others were afraid her baby would suffer if she went out or stood on her feet too long. That cut it down to three: Thatch, Floy and Karen.

On the fifth day of rain, Karen took a hand. "Your turn to go out," she said to Gus.

"What?" Gus seemed not to understand.

"What if something happened to Thatch? We all have to know our way around," Karen said persuasively.

"I can't go out! It's raining!"

"Why so it is," Karen said as if surprised. "You had better take off your clothes so they won't get wet."

"No!" Gus said, sounding shocked.

Karen stripped, ready for the rain. "I will not return until you fetch me," she said, and stepped out.

Gus stared after her. "This is ridiculous," he said. It was all Zena could do to keep from laughing, for he was now using her own phrase. "Thatch, bring her back!"

Thatch headed for the door, but Zena stopped him. "This is between the two of them," she said.

The door opened. Gus whirled around—but it was Floy, not Karen. "Something up?" she asked as she shook the water off her bare torso. "It's not Karen's turn to walk out, but she told me—"

Zena brought a towel and dried her off. The girl did have a good young figure, and getting better as she grew, but she still was almost intolerably clumsy. It was better to help her than to let her bash about doing things for herself. "She says its Gus's turn," Zena murmured.

"Oh." Floy glanced at Gus, comprehending. "Good for her." Then her eyes fell upon the blonde wig Gordon had used, and something went out of her. She picked it up, crossed to the driver's seat, and sat down.

For an hour Gus paced about the bus, muttering. No one else spoke. Zena could tell by his reactions the hold Karen had over him. There was a lot of woman out there in the rain!

Thatch took Gordon's old shirt over to Floy. Karen had laundered the blood out of it and dried it as well as possible. He put it over the girl's still shoulders, then took the adjacent seat. The members of the group were closer now, drawn together by the common tragedy of Gordon's death. In the same fashion the others took care of Zena, they now took care of Floy. Yet it would have been infinitely better had Gordon lived.

At last Gus launched himself out into the rain. "Karen! Karen!" he called. "Come back!"

As though she had just left.

Floy looked back, the wig on her head: incongruous,

156

because Zena was so used to the features of Gloria, the statuesque blonde, not this pinched child's face, prematurely aged by grief. "It won't work," she said, and returned to her private reflections.

Floy had had nobody, until Gordon. What would she do, what would she be, when she came out of her sorrow? Was there hope for her now?

Fifteen minutes later Karen showed up. "I need help," she said.

Now Thatch went out. When they returned, they were supporting Gus, who was blubbering with fear. They got him inside and put him on the back couch, soaking clothes and all.

"I thought he could do it," Karen said, shaking her head sadly. "But the moment the rain hit him, he collapsed. He's terrified of falling water. He never got beyond the wall of the bus."

Zena shook her head. It was hard to believe that a man could be such a coward, but it made things fall into place. Gus did not boss Thatch because he was stronger, but because he was weak. "At least he tried," Zena said.

Time passed. Their deck of cards became worn, and the books were read and reread. Zena went through every page of the *Whole Earth Catalog*, knowing that it was largely an exercise in futility. The Earth was no longer whole, and none of these intriguing things could now be ordered. She was morbidly fascinated by the section on childbirth . . . followed by the one on death.

She wished she could go outside. But she had to content herself with doing calisthenics for health.

Thatch ranged more widely in his search for supplies. He reported that the rain was now eroding the forest land, forming huge new gullies. The paint had been scoured from the outside of the bus.

One day, about a month into Mindel, he came back shaken. "I found their other camp," he said.

"The attackers?" Zena asked.

157

"Yes. They had a home base about five miles from here, shored up with rocks. For their women and children."

Zena felt the ugly, familiar chill. "Children?"

"They had too little food, inadequate shelter. They're gone now."

"Children!" Zena exclaimed. "They wanted the bus for the children!"

Thatch nodded. "It looks as if there were six men, five women, and six children of different ages. I saw their skeletons."

"Skeletons!"

"They were out in the open. Their roof had collapsed, maybe after they were dead. The wild animals, the rain. . . ."

"They must have needed the bus more than we did!"

"They attacked us!" Gus said. "What could we do?"

"If I had known," Zena said.

"They could have talked to us," Floy said. "We might have taken the children—if they had only asked. But they came instead to rape and kill. So what happened, happened."

And that was true. There *had* been occasion for negotiation, when Gloria fetched water for the first man. But the others had cared only for deceit and violence—and had paid the awful price. And Gordon was dead.

The Biblical forty days of the first rain had passed, but this time there was no abatement. Their carefully rationed meat diminished; what they did not eat rapidly enough, the fungus did. There was no hope of lasting out Mindel on their present supplies.

"Only two ways to eat," Gus said. "First, go out and kill more people. . . ."

"That isn't even funny," Zena said. But she was as concerned as any, for the baby inside her was growing large.

"Second, we have to go fishing again."

And those strange, vicious fish would now be much larger and more irritable, and the constant storm would make the job several times as hard. But what else was there?

They thrashed it out and decided. Gus would stay behind in the bus, for it could not be driven now. Zena would come, and Floy, and Foundling; Dust Devil would stay with Gus.

"Remember, Gus," Karen said. "If the bus is taken over, they'll throw you out in the rain."

Gus nodded. He looked terrified, and Zena felt perverse sympathy for him. Some people were afraid of rain, others of sex. A lot could be tolerated when its exact nature was appreciated. Not understood, not condoned, but tolerated, and that was sufficient.

Still, it was ironic that awkward Floy, who could have stood guard well, was coming to haul on the net while big strong Gus, afraid of being alone, would stay behind.

The complete net was far too bulky to carry, so Thatch fitted a smaller section in his pack. Any fish at all would be better than none.

The descent was horrendous. This was the first occasion Zena had been out for any extended trip since Mindel began falling, and the rain was much stronger than before. She found it hard to breathe, feeling as though she were under water. It was foggy, too, so that visibility was further limited. Not only was the footing treacherous, the landscape had changed drastically. Erosion gullies had become minor canyons. Loud torrents of water smashed down the mountain. It was impossible to cross these; they could toss whole trees about and sunder them unnoticed. A puny human body would be instantly lost.

Karen put her mouth to Thatch's ear and yelled something. Thatch nodded agreement. He unwound the coil of rope he carried and went to each of them in turn, looping it about their middles. He hesitated before Zena, and she knew why: he was afraid of injuring the developing baby. "If I die, it dies too," she yelled. "That's the point of this whole expedition. Tie the rope!"

So he tied it, still doubtful. They went on, linked like mountain climbers: Thatch in the lead, Karen second, Floy third, and Zena at the rear.

As they descended, the mist became thicker in patches, seeming to flow down in rivers of its own. At its worst, it obscured everything beyond a few feet. They had to go slowly, because it was possible to step into a slippery gully they could not get out of.

Even so, the scenery was phenomenal. Sheer canyon walls loomed, seeming taller than they were because the mist shrouded the upper reaches. Zena was sure the rain could not have made these so quickly; they must be faults in the structure of the mountains, formerly hidden, now exposed by the washing away of the covering dirt and gravel.

Yet not everything had been scoured. The fungus and mildew and moss—whatever the stuff was that she had noted during the dry period—had now multiplied fantastically. The lower and partially sheltered regions were thick with mushrooms. Zena did not know whether the nutrients in the alien water fertilized this explosive growth, or whether the plant growth thrived on sediments from the catastrophic erosion, but thrive it did. Branches and trunks of trees were coated with moss, in some cases inches deep; rocks were transformed into greenish mounds; and even portions of the ground had become a resilient living carpet. The stuff was slippery when squashed, so that she was always afraid of falling. It had a vile smell when bruised.

But Thatch had explored all this region thoroughly, noting the changes as they occurred, and he knew where he was going. Zena was appalled in retrospect, now that she saw the immensity of the ongoing changes. Thatch could have been killed any one of those days of exploration, leaving the others in the bus helpless. No one, however brave or strong, could hope to survive long here without the kind of knowledge Thatch had evolved.

No, not quite true, she reminded herself. Karen had come out here, and Floy. Still, why had none of them told her about this?

She knew the answer to that too. Because they had not wanted to worry her. Because of the baby.

They stepped down into a stream bed. There was very little water here, and Zena wondered why. Most other channels were raging torrents. Then they came to a fault traversing it, and she understood: all the rushing water was being diverted into the lower crevices, leaving this one comparatively high and dry. But woe betide whoever fell into one of the nether reaches!

They stepped carefully over the cross-fault, hearing the roar of subterranean rapids, smelling the spray from the river. The ground shuddered here, making Zena fearful that the entire section of rock on which they walked would momentarily break off and plunge into that awful abyss.

Her pregnancy had turned her into a silly weak woman. She would have to do something about that!

Then a scramble up a rocky incline, under a lone tree that clung to its diminished plot of earth, and down another crevice. For a moment the fog lifted, owing to some peculiarity of the draft, and Zena could see where they were going. It was like a landscape of Mars, with holes like craters and faults like crevices. Or perhaps more like Venus, considering the cloud cover.

Thatch stopped abruptly. "Oh-oh," he said. "Something new."

At first Zena did not see what he meant. Then she smelled stronger fumes, something like burning sulfur. And felt warmth—not the mild warmth of the rain, but of a furnace.

161

Hot steam was issuing from a vent in the nearby rock. It hissed like an irate dragon.

"That was not here two days ago," Thatch said worriedly.

"Is this a volcanic area?" Karen asked.

"No."

Zena felt the unpleasant prickle of fear run up her back. "How can it be hot, if—" But she was able to answer that herself. "The subterranean rock is always hot. If a fissure reached down far enough—"

Thatch nodded. "The ocean must be two or three hundred feet above its original level by now. That is a lot of pressure on the land. Enough to push it in, make cracks, force the layers to buckle. Earthquakes—"

"Minor compared to what must be going on in the true volcanic regions." Zena said. "But it certainly makes me nervous here!"

"Nothing we can do but go on," Karen said. "We'll have to keep an eye on it for the next few days, however. If steam starts coming up under the bus—"

Zena shivered. "You *would* think of that!"

They continued on over the nightmare terrain. It took two hours to reach the sea—less time than Zena had expected. Then she realized why: the sea was much closer than it had been.

"It's not the sea," Thatch said, realizing what they were thinking. "It's the Tennessee Valley Lake—the same one we went to before. Much higher and closer now. But before this rain is done, it *will* be the sea."

They anchored the near side of the net to trees that had not yet been drowned or washed out, and flung the rest into the water. There was no concern about man-eaters here, but there was an obvious current.

Then the bait; chopped-up fragments of human bone and tendon. They let these sink, and waited half an hour for the fish to discover the delicacies and gather. The the-

162

ory was that the aromas would spread through the water and alert any hungry lake denizens within range.

At length they hauled it in. There were a few small bony fish that looked unhealthy.

Zena sighed. "I know it's not much of a day and not much of a net, but somehow I expected better."

"This is a new lake," Karen said. "The creatures we saw last time must have been a passing phase, and there hasn't been time for a new population to develop. The original spawning beds must have been washed out. This rain is as hard on the fish as on us!"

Floy had been idly digging in the soaking ground with a stick. She was making a fair hole, since all it took was energy and she wasn't aiming for any specific place. "Look!" she said.

It was a fat grub. "Bait," Karen said.

"I was thinking of food," Floy said. "Must be a lot of these in the ground. It's so wet and warm—"

Zena made a face, but Karen took the matter seriously. "You're right, Floy! Grubs, worms, insects—wherever there is some protected dirt, they must be multiplying explosively. If we could eat them, we would never have to stray far from home."

"Not so fast!" Zena said. "There is very little protected dirt on this mountain. This is a recent alluvial deposit—material carried down by the water as it slows to enter the lake. You can tell, because there is no moss on it. You won't find similar deposits near the bus. And the grubs can't be everywhere; probably this one was carried down with the dirt and only survived by chance."

Thatch looked at the few small fish they had netted. "I can come down here alone each day and bring back a few."

"Fish and grubs," Karen said. "It won't be much, but maybe enough to tide us through until the ocean arrives."

"I'd as soon eat the moss," Zena said. Then she lifted her

head, startled at the notion. "The moss—if we could eat *that*—"

"But the smell!" Floy protested, wrinkling her nose. Her lip pulled up as she did it, reminding Zena that Floy's coordination problems were not over.

"What about the smell of some kinds of cheese?" Zena asked. "They smell like stale urine. So do some wines— and they look the part, too! We could acquire the taste, if there were enough food value."

Karen nodded. "You may have a point. Let's try some."

"It might be poisonous," Floy said.

Karen harvested a handful of green from the nearest rock. "Possible, but the odds are against it. This stuff hasn't been around long enough to have natural enemies, so shouldn't have defenses against them. And its odor may do that job anyway." She put the stuff to her mouth. "But if it *is* deadly, there's only one way to find out." She took a bite.

The others watched in apprehensive silence while she chewed. "Uh, awful!" Karen said. But she took another mouthful.

"Maybe it would taste better if you cooked it," Zena suggested. "Cooking changes onions, rhubarb—"

"Could be," Karen agreed. "If we got rid of the present flavor, then spiced it up with other things."


Cooking did help some, and spices some more; but mainly they just had to acquire a taste for the green growth. Karen's digestion did not suffer, so they deemed it fit for human consumption. Once they had accepted the notion of eating the foul stuff, it was like manna from heaven. Instead of fishing, Thatch went out foraging for superior flavors of moss; there were several varieties. The menu was dull, but it kept them alive when all other food was gone.

The rain continued; two months, three months, four.

Wurm had now had time to join Mindel and Riss, prolonging the deluge. The water scoured the exterior of the bus and dug out the ground beneath it. Every day they shoveled material back in to shore it up, and carried the largest rocks they could handle, but it was a losing battle against the indefatigable elements. If the rain did not abate soon, the bus would start its slide down the mountain. Already the palisade was gone, and Gordon's grave, and all the wood that had not been tied together and anchored to the bus.

Thatch was always punctual—until the day he did not return. "The terrain could have changed," Karen said. "Maybe the roof of a river caved in, and he has to circle back the long way."

"Maybe he's hurt," Gus said. "Somebody should go after him."

Not Gus himself, obviously. And not Floy; her coordination would merely get her in trouble, too. And Zena was now six months pregnant.

"I agree," Karen said. "And I am the one. But there's something you should know."

"We know it," Floy said. "You're out of insulin."

Zena was horrified. She had buried the knowledge that Karen's time was running out, and had almost convinced herself that the crisis would never come. "Oh, no!" she cried. "Is that true?"

"True. I have been rationing it, but there are limits. I have enough for only a few more days. I have been able to function well enough because I have not been eating much. But if I have to go out in that storm, I need to be fully alert—and that means eating a big meal and using all my remaining supply in one dose."

"No," Zena said firmly. "You can't do that."

"I'm not making excuses," Karen said. "I have been resigned to my situation for some time. The number of days remaining is less important than the use to which they are put. I had hoped to be on hand to help with the baby; now I know that is not to be. I think I ought to go look for Thatch; you need him for survival. But if I fail—"

Gus had seemed not to understand the nature of the dialogue. Now he came to Karen. "You'll be all right," he said reassuringly. "You don't need that stuff. Maybe a few days withdrawal pains . . ."

"Maybe so," Karen agreed with a half-smile.

Zena exchanged glances with Floy. Both knew that the end of the insulin meant the end of Karen. Gus was fooling himself, and Karen was going along, rather than aggravate the situation. It was easier—for everyone—if the truth were suppressed—until the end.

"Come on back," Gus said.

Karen went with him. Zena was disgusted.

"What is it like?" Floy asked, watching them go. "I can see Karen likes it. Gordon said I was a child, so he never . . ." Her face clouded up, as it did whenever she remembered Gordon, and she was unable to continue.

"I can't tell you," Zena said. "I only did it to get pregnant; I never felt anything." Except discomfort, she added mentally, and disgust.

"You're such a damn prude!" Floy cried.

Zena slapped her, hard.

The reaction was unthinking, but she did not regret it. They had been cooped up for a long time. The nerve of this child!

Zena had half expected Floy to burst into tears, but the girl reacted like her fighting cat. She crouched, flung back her wild hair, and raised fingers like claws.

Zena remembered that eyeball, and suddenly she was afraid.

Then Floy relaxed. "Aw, you can't help it," she said with infinite scorn.

Zena found herself crying. That one sentence defined her so accurately! There was something seriously wrong with her reactions to men, and she couldn't help it. She was as crippled as Floy, or Karen, or Gus.

Where was Thatch? Without him the group was surely doomed! Karen was the only other really competent member, and she would soon be gone.

Zena was carrying Thatch's baby. Surely that meant something. What would be the fate of that infant if its father died?

Could Thatch be dead already? There were a thousand perils in that deluge. Every day the landscape changed; now torrents cut through new channels, tore out new chunks of acreage. And the strange new insects were multiplying, many of them huge and slick, at home in the rain but hungry for blood. If he had blundered into a nest of Mindel hornets. . . .

"I must find him," Zena said.

Floy moved over to the door, barring the way. "You can't. Karen's the only one can do it."

"I must." Zena approached the door. "Move—or be moved."

Again that catlike crouch, the bared claws. They were all overreacting to the slightest stimuli, ready to duel on any pretext, yet the aggressive forms had to be honored. Zena saw herself as much as victim as Floy—and yet would not yield.

"I'm sorry we fought," Floy said. "But we need that baby. There may never be another in this world. You're staying here."

Did the girl appreciate the ironies? No matter! Zena drew her knife. The blade was sharp and the point hung inches from Floy's face. "I'm sorry too," she said. "But I will not be balked by a child." She was not certain which child she meant.

Again Floy relaxed. "I guess not," she said. "But I'd better come with you."

Strange girl! But she had backed off when that was

167

necessary, showing good judgment. "If *I* can't find him, how could *you?*"

"It's not him I'm thinking of."

"Well, why don't you think of what's inside the bus? If Thatch is lost, and I don't come back, in a few days there'll be only one possible source for a baby." Dirty fighting, but a point that had to be made sometime.

Floy's eyes widened. "God, yes!" she said.

Zena went on down and out. The rain hit her like the blast of a waterfall, knocking her back against the bus. The tempo had increased! It was now four of five times as great as the rate during the Gunz deluge. Mighty Mindel, whose strength was as the strength of . . . never mind! She opened her mouth to breathe, and the liquid poured in. She spat it out and tried to breathe through her nose, but that was worse.

Finally she dropped her head and sucked in air through her teeth. She shaded her eyes with one hand, peering about. The rain and fog were so dense it seemed like night; effective visibility was ten or twelve feet. The ground was all water.

She went out in it, treading carefully to find the rock inches beneath her, making her stagger. One foot landed in an unseeable hole, and she fell.

She was unhurt, but fear for her baby made her decide that for the time being four feet were better than two. She proceeded to the edge of the level area that had been the palisade enclosure. Here the water streamed away downhill, disappearing into the misty ambience.

"Thatch! Thatch!" she cried, but her voice was lost in the roar of storm and rapids. How could she ever find him?

She scrambled on, clinging to whatever offered. There had been a time when she could have managed such travel well despite the barrage of water, but now she was six months along.

A stone gave way. Suddenly she was rolling helplessly,

carried along by gravity and the flow of water. The roaring grew louder, signaling the proximity of a cataract, therefore her demise.

"Thatch!" she cried while choking on water. Her voice as she heard it sounded the way Gus's had, that first time he had been hurt at the start of this adventure. Had she sunk so low! Then: "I love you!"

She splashed into a deep pool, flailing wildly, bobbed to the surface and gasped for air. A current was bearing her along somewhere, so she fought it. Her hand caught hold of something and held.

The water was not cold, and it shielded her from the force of the rain, so she remained where she was while she assessed her situation. What was a pool doing *here?* There should be nothing but erosion gullies and canyons.

Silly question! The contours of the land were changing so drastically that no new feature should be surprising. She was lucky she wasn't dead.

Yet.

Still, she had not found Thatch—physically. But emotionally—had she meant it? Had the truth come out at last, that she had twisted her way unwillingly into love with the father of her child? Was that why she had faced down Floy and braved Mindel to seek him out?

Now she wasn't sure. It was easy to love, when there was no future in it. What about the reality, the giving of one's whole being to another? Could she ever do that?

Of only one thing was she certain: she could no longer exist without him.

Now she just had to find him. She swam around the rocky edge of the pool, seeking a suitable place to climb out.

There was none. The stone was either slick underneath the flowing water, or covered with slimy lichen that broke away in handfuls, providing no purchase. The slope was too steep to permit her to climb out independently.

She was not hurt; a few stinging scrapes were all the

wounds she had sustained in her tumble. She was not cold, or sick. But she was caught, and probably doomed, for she could not tread water forever.

She had caught hold of something, during her first flailings. Where was it now?

She swam back, rechecking carefully. Under the greenery was the root of a tree, invisible from the water but still solid. The tree itself was gone, but the root seemed firm. She hauled on it.

The thing came loose in her hand. It was only a half-buried piece, dislodged by her efforts.

"Zena!"

It was Thatch, out of sight but close by.

"Here!" she cried.

"In the pond?"

"Yes!"

"I'll send down the rope."

And the end of the rope came down; she located it by the faint splash into the water, hardly distinguishable from the continuous splash of rain. She caught and pulled herself up, hand over hand, sliding on her fat belly over the moss. It was not far; the same slipperiness that had trapped her, now made the travel easier. So long as her feet were able to punch through to find purchase.

Thatch caught her arm at the leveling of the bank. He stood her on her feet. "Floy said you had gone out," he said.

"I was afraid—" But her fears seemed foolish, in the face of his obvious health. "I'm sorry."

"I'm glad I found you! If anything had happened—"

"Aren't you going to bawl me out? For getting in trouble?"

"I don't understand."

No, he wouldn't. Thatch never blamed anyone for anything, however culpable others might be. "So you know why I came out?"

"Yes."

170

She hesitated. "You *do?*"

"Floy told me."

Zena suffered a flash of anger. "What did Floy tell you?"

"We'd better get back."

"She told you that?"

"No." Verbal plays were still wasted on him; he always answered literally. "But it isn't safe for you to stay out here."

"What did she tell you?"

He paused, but then answered. "That you love me."

Zena clenched her teeth. *Why couldn't she have said it herself?* Was it really easier to get pregnant by a man, than to tell him she loved him?

"I know the way back," Thatch said.

She went with him, wordlessly.

# Chapter 8: Labor

Karen was haggard. Her normally rounded body had turned gaunt, though she ate reasonably and drank insatiably. She seemed drowsy and very tired, and her breath smelled fruity. Often she retreated to the bathroom to urinate copiously—then gulped more water. This aggravated Zena almost intolerably, but she knew its cause and kept silent. The water was needed to dilute the rampant sugar in her blood—the sugar that could not get to the cells of the body where it was so badly needed. The diabetes was now uncontrolled, for the last of the insulin was gone.

Gus was now alarmed. "Snap out of it, Karen! Can't I help you?" he asked plaintively, again and again.

Karen only shook her head. Her breathing was deep and labored, and her skin was flushed yet dry. She seemed to have aged, and not graciously; her beauty was gone.

"I'm going out and find some insulin," Gus said, marching to the door. But there he stopped, balked by his fear of the rain. And as he paused uncertainly, there was a violent shudder in the ground that rattled the plates on the table and made everyone jump.

"Another fissure opening up," Floy said. "Maybe a volcano."

"Ridiculous!" Zena said. But it wasn't really. Not any more. With the enormous pressure of the sea water building up, and the erosion of the counterweight of soil and gravel, intolerable stresses were building. The world, like Karen, was sick; like her, it was developing awful symptoms that seemed paradoxical.

Gus still stood by the door. "You can't go out," Zena told him, feeling like a hypocrite for justifying his inability to act. "Where in this flooded world would there be any insulin?"

There was another shudder, and this time they heard the boom of some great explosion. "*Must* be a volcano," Floy said. "Crack Toe."

Gus turned. "You mean Krakatoa."

"Right. Crack Toe," she repeated. "Smithereens."

Even Karen smiled, wanly.

"It can't make very much difference to us," Zena said, though she knew that she was being unduly pessimistic, as they should be able to survive the rain, provided the tremors did not dump them all into a crevasse. But with Karen dying. . . .

Karen rested quietly for a time. Then she sat up and vomited. Zena stifled her own nausea and cleaned up as well as she could. Another earth tremor made her take a spill, so that she had to do the job twice, but that seemed fitting. Maybe the world itself was sharing Karen's suffering.

But the patient saw it another way. "You're making me suffer," Karen muttered as the heaves abated. "Just a little pressure on the carotid arteries—you know where to do it, Zena."

173

"No!" Zena cried.

"Painless, out like a light," Karen continued weakly. "After that, it doesn't matter how. Cut my throat, catch the blood in a basin—"

"God!" Gus said.

"You'd be doing me a favor. And the meat would be better. It's spoiling right now." She took a breath. "Promise me you won't waste the meat."

"We won't," Zena said.

At last Karen lapsed into a tortured sleep. So did the others: it had not been possible while the woman agonized.

The loud rain continued—and so did the booms of the burgeoning volcano. Once Zena got heaved onto the floor, and the entire bus shifted position alarmingly. Zena merely crawled back onto the bed and slept again.

When she woke, someone had covered Karen's face with a sheet.

"It is time to take her out," Floy said.

Thatch stooped to pick up Karen's body. "Let her be!" Gus said.

Thatch hesitated. "No," Floy said. "She wanted it as it was with Gordon. To help the group, to preserve the baby. It would not be right to waste her. And we promised."

"That's right," Zena agreed grimly. "I'll help. It must be done."

"Not with her!" Gus protested, his body shaking. "I love her!"

"I loved Gordon," Floy said. "But I ate him."

Thatch made another motion to pick up the body. Gus lunged to stop him—and Floy leaped on Gus. He cried out in pain. Two bloody streaks appeared across his forehead. "Thatch!" he screamed. "I'm hurt!"

Zena put a hand on Thatch's shoulder. "She knows what she's doing," she murmured. She remembered how Floy

174

had refrained from fighting, when Zena herself had challenged her; that had been judgment, not fear.

Thatch looked back and forth indecisively. "Gus—"

"Gus can't keep a corpse in here," Zena said. "He needs a woman."

Thatch looked at Floy. The girl was lean and hollow-eyed from her own mourning. Her hair was long and wild, and her claws were showing. She was like a hungry tigress, but her dynamism gave her a certain sex appeal. And Gus had always had a certain hankering . . .

"And I need a man," Zena said. "I think I could love a man. An independent man."

Still Thatch hesitated, unable to break his long symbiosis with Gus. It was this more than anything else, Zena realized, that really stood between herself and Thatch. A physical homosexuality would have disgusted her; this emotional mutualism acted more subtly to inhibit other attachments.

At last Thatch nodded. He bent again to pick up the body. "Thatch!" Gus cried again, but Thatch ignored him. He hauled Karen's corpse off the couch and down the hall toward the door.

Gus tried once more to interfere, but halted as Floy came at him. "I can do what she did," Floy said. "I know how you feel. I've been through it all." She spoke with a low intensity that showed she meant it.

They got the body outside. Zena glanced back, unable to restrain her morbid curiosity. Gus and Floy were already on the back couch, in an embrace of antagonism or of passion. Probably some of each—but it was what was required at that moment.

The rain blasted down, instantly matting the hair over the dead woman's face and obscuring visibility. "That girl's got courage," Zena said. Actually she was yelling, to get over the noise of Mindel.

"So have you," Thatch called back.

He dumped down the body. Zena couldn't even tell

175

whether it splashed, because everything was a splash out here. She had the sheet, and now laid it over the face.

Thatch drew his knife. Zena held Karen's hair tightly while Thatch cut around the neck. The sheet concealed the sight of what they were doing, and the rain washed away any blood there might have been before it showed. It should not have been wasted—but there were limits.

"So have you," Zena said, averting her gaze anyway.

"She showed me how," he said, misunderstanding her comment.

There was another tremor, a violent one. The corpse jumped into the air. Zena screamed involuntarily, and Thatch jerked back. His glasses flew off his head; they had been anchored by a chain around the back of his head, but this must have broken.

Even through the thick rain they saw it: the flare of Crack Toe letting go. The falling water turned red, and Zena thought she saw a halo from the refraction. Then the sound came, as of a mountain being torn apart.

Slowly the sight and sound faded. Zena's attention returned to things nearby. "Your glasses!" she cried.

Thatch held them up. The lenses had been shattered.

"Can you see without them?" she asked.

He nodded. "Well enough—close range. You are beautiful."

"That's well enough," she said. Why this coy banter, amidst the most grisly business of butchering a friend? Was she losing her grip on reality?

They returned to work. The head jerked and rolled with the force of cutting. It felt like a living thing, struggling to get free. Zena vomited into the storm, but did not relinquish her hold. It had to be done.

After an interminable time the head came away. Zena lifted it by the hair and forced herself to look. It was no longer Karen, but the mask of a stranger, severed at the neck. Still, she knew that some of the water streaming down her face was tears. If only there had been some other way. . . .

Zena wrapped it carefully in the sheet and set it on the step of the bus, just inside the door. "We'd better do the rest now," she said. "While I'm still heaved out."

They removed Karen's clothing and Thatch took up the knife again. But the blade trembled. "I can't carve a woman!" he said miserably.

Zena looked down at the headless corpse and saw what he meant. The head had been a necessary thing, and he had done that before. Now a beautifully feminine torso was exposed. Only a certain type of man would be able to mutilate those attributes, and Thatch was not that type.

Gus normally bullied Thatch into finding a way. Zena was not going to do that; she wanted such bullying to stop. "I'll start it," she said. She knew that once the body had been defeminized, Thatch would be able to continue. He would have to, because Zena lacked the physical strength to sever the bones and tissues of that body.

She took the knife. It was glistening and clean, for the rain scoured it constantly. She gritted her teeth and made an incision. The blade was sharp, and it was like cutting meat—unsurprisingly. Then she retched again, her stomach knotting. But there was no escape in sickness; this job, like every job since the first rain started, had to be done.

She carved. Through much of it her eyes were closed, but she kept going.

When she was done she turned the blade over to Thatch.

She saw a discoloration on his teeth and knew that he too had been puking. She reached out to catch his hand, touched by this first sign of genuine weakness in him. She brought it to her lips for a wet kiss.

Then they both leaned over the body from opposite sides and kissed each other on the lips. It was the first time, for even in the sexual embrace she had always turned her face away. It was unutterably sweet.

177

There was no refuge from the horror of Karen's demise but love. With love they could continue. Zena knew that this feeling, so long and hard in coming, would never depart.

Zena held while Thatch carved. It was a long, difficult, awful job—but her spirit glowed with that transcendent emotion, and time was nothing. She loved Thatch—and through him Floy, and even Gus, and Karen and Gordon, and Dust Devil and Foundling . . . and herself. Love.

At last they were done, all but the smoking of the new meat. They reentered the bus, to find Floy and Gus recovered. Zena kissed Floy, then Gus, and returned to Thatch, and nothing needed to be said.

"Do you think Karen's spirit is with Gordon now?" Floy asked.

Zena had to set aside her own returned misery while she considered the ramifications of the question. What would be the right answer? "Karen was a good woman," she said. "A brave, good woman. Gordon was a good man, and he has been alone long enough. It is only right that they be together. They have to do what is best in their life, just as we must in ours."

"That's beautiful," Floy said. "I am not jealous now."

Then, as once before, they were hugging each other, expressing in tears the emotions that could not be properly conveyed in words.


Now they were four, and the two animals. Thatch continued to forage for edible moss, and Zena carved and cooked the meat in small portions. The rain went on, and the noise and motion of the volcano.

At five months of the Mindel deluge, something under the bus collapsed. They tumbled out of bed, alarmed. Zena, seven months pregnant, clung to the furniture while Thatch leaped down the steps to check outside.

"Foundation's gone!" he yelled. "The whole area's been

undermined. The bus is falling into a sink hole! The next 'quake will—"

"We've got to get out!" Zena cried. "If we get stuck in an underground cavity, we'll never survive the rain!" She had thought the worst was over when Karen died; now she knew that none of them had any guarantee of survival.

"It can go any time," Thatch said. "Jam everything you can into the packs and get out in a minute or two! I know where we can find temporary shelter."

Zena packed feverishly. She didn't bother with clothing, but concentrated on useful items: the knives, tools, rope and remaining smoked meat. She tossed the first pack out to Thatch, and worked on another. Floy made a quick, clumsy search of the closets and cupboards, pointing out the essentials. Gus just stared.

"Okay—out!" Zena cried, leading the way. The bus shifted again, terrifying her as it added emphasis to the directive.

"I can't!" Gus cried.

Floy showed him her claws. "Move!" she yelled.

She herded him like a frightened stallion, forcing him to the steps and down. Gus screamed as the rain struck him—but fear of the little beast behind him forced him on. They scrabbled out of the depression the bus was in following Thatch in a circuitous but secure route. Dust Devil hated the rain almost as much as Gus did, but bounded after Foundling on a parallel route.

Once clear of the bus they stopped to link up with the rope. Thatch took the lead, with Zena second; then Gus, and Floy right behind him. Gus's eyes were tightly closed; only the tug of the rope and Floy's screeched directions got him moving in the right direction. They forged on through the torrent, a motley party.

Thatch guided them to a rocky overhang. The water had undercut it, then changed course; now the stone offered partial shelter. "This is solid," Thatch said. "And there're several routes away from it."

Gus huddled against the stone wall, taking no other interest in survival.

"There are still trees and rocks," Floy said. "We'll have to build our own shelter, here. And a covered fireplace, so we can cook. Gus and I will fetch in rocks; can't have Zena lifting too much."

Zena was angry at the girl's assumptions, but realized after a moment that she was witnessing a promising phenomenon. The clumsy child, so recently become an effective woman, was now stepping into the leadership breach. Zena was unable to do that, especially in her present condition, and Thatch was not the type. Gus was a loss. If Floy could do it, why protest?

But could Floy do it? Gus seemed to be a lost cause.

"Come on, Gus," Floy said. "You have more muscles than any of us; show us what you can carry."

Gus did not move. Exposure to the storm had completely inactivated him.

Floy went to kneel beside him. "Now I'm going to show you three things," she said gently. "First, the intellectual: we need your help, because Zena's getting near baby-time, and Thatch has to forage where only he can go, and I just don't have the ability to pick up a big slippery rock and move it. If you don't pitch in, it won't get done—and we'll never get out of this rain, and we'll die here like Gordon and Karen, and have to eat each other, one by one, and you'll be the last to go, and you'll be alone in the rain."

"No!" Gus cried in terror.

"Second, a promise," Floy said. She tore off her soaking clothing to reveal her slender but rather attractively developed body. "The moment we have shelter, you and I are going to have a lot of fun, you know what kind."

That disgusted Zena—but not the way it once might have. It was evident that it was a very real inducement to Gus, who had always admired Floy's body and had had recent experience of its potentials. Even Thatch was looking at Floy with male appreciation. Sex, obviously, always loomed large in the interests of men, and now it was an excellent tool. Perhaps that was why men had been evolved with the desire, the women with the appeal. If women had craved it as men did, they would never have been able to use it effectively.

"Third," Floy continued, "if you do not move this instant I will give you this." And she flicked one finger out from her palm, the long nail gleaming. The effect was like the sudden opening of a switchblade, right under Gus's nose. The nail made a little quiver, as of an incipient thrust at the man's left eye, and Gus hurled himself away and into the rain.

Floy did have the necessary qualities of leadership!


Zena lay under the shelter, feeling the pangs of what threatened to be forthcoming labor. "But it is only eight months!" she cried. "Too soon. Too soon!"

Floy came to sit beside her. In the past month of industry, the girl had grown subtly. Her coordination had become almost normal, and there was an air of competence about her that was reassuring. Of all the group, she had adapted best to the necessities of Mindel. "How do you know?" Floy asked.

"I kept count!"

"You started with Thatch just after Gunz."

"That was ten months ago!" Zena sounded shrill in her own ears.

"Right. So it could be nine months now for the baby, or even overdue. Why worry about it?"

"It's *eight* months! I know. I don't want it premature!"

Floy had learned not to argue with unreasonable women. "I'll get you some green soup."

"Who's going to deliver the baby?" Zena cried. "I wish Karen were here . . . or even Gloria."

"Karen is here—in spirit. Her body is part of ours, part of your baby's too. She makes us strong, the same way. Gloria, too."

Floy's only moments of weakness were still when she remembered Gordon. Now it was only a pause, a silence, a moment of rather pretty sadness.

Then something made them both listen, startled. "What is it?" Zena demanded.

"The rain's stopping!" Floy cried. "Mindel's down! And Ring Riss, and Ringworm . . ."

"Ringworm!" Zena echoed, and started laughing uncontrollably. Floy joined her. Together they lay and looked out of the rock shelter, weak from foolish mirth.

They crawled out and looked at the sky. A huge band of cloud remained, but the configuration had changed. To the south the sky was clear; to the north it looked as though the rain continued.

"The whole canopy is drifting into the polar opening," Zena said. "There's not enough vapor left to support the full cloud cover!"

"We made it through!" Floy said. "We made it!"

In a moment they heard a halloo, and Gus came charging up the mountain slope. "The rain stopped!" he yelled unnecessarily.

They waited for Thatch, then commenced an exploration of the post-canopy world. It was spectacular, now that the fog had lifted and the slanting sunlight touched the earth. Zena had to shield her eyes, unused to the direct sunlight for six months and more. The glare seemed intolerable at first, but she squinted happily.

Little vegetation of the old style remained, for the rain had washed out roots and soil. But the new moss that clung to rock was luxuriant, coating every partially protected surface with green and gray and brown.

The hardest rock had held up; but anything susceptible to erosion by water or gravel had been cleaned out. Gullies like the Grand Canyon opened below their residence.

182

And the new volcanism had altered the landscape in its own fashion. Steam issued from cracks in the stone, and the water that flowed near these vents was hot.

To the west, Crack Toe smoked calmly. This was the first time they had actually seen it. Zena was almost disappointed to find that it was a rather small development, not even properly conical. It was a gap in the side of a regular mountain, with a dribble of solidified lava trailing beneath it. Who would have believed that all that noise and motion could have emanated from that!

Below was the ocean—the real ocean, now. They stood on an island a few miles across, surrounded by other islands: the tops of the former Appalachians. All the rest of the world had been drowned.

They picked their way down to that great sea, two thousand feet above the level of the old one. Already the moss was beginning to wither, as it was dependent on the thorough moisture of the rain and fog. But there was no concern about food; there was life in the ocean. Apparently the fish had adapted to the breakup of their spawning grounds and the dilution of the salt water and had multiplied during the storm.

Zena marveled at that. She had thought the limits were much narrower. For one thing, she had understood that much sea life was dependent on direct sunlight. But she could think of two explanations: first, that there had been many quick extinctions, as in ages past, leaving room for those better able to cope with the changed environment. Second, that this type of thing had indeed happened before, so that the creatures of the sea had prior experience. No doubt there had been an explosion of the fungus life in the sea as well as on land, providing an alternate source of food. Fungus was independent of light, so it was always ready to fill the vacuum.

What had happened to the fishes of the sea at the time of Noah's flood? Geologically, this was still soon after that

183

deluge. The sea creatures would not have forgotten, genetically, how to handle it.

In addition, the warmth of the water, plus the wealth of refuse washed down from land, had provided an ideal growth medium for those species ready to take advantage of it. The net would feed the little party of four people and two animals indefinitely.

"The world is ours," Gus said, pleased. His whole personality seemed to have sprung back the moment the rain stopped. Had he already sealed off the deluge as a nightmare?

A sinuous ripple approached. It was an alligator, a large one. The reptiles, like the fish, were doing well!

"This warm weather, and all that water," Zena murmured. "The cold-blooded creatures thrive on it. The world is really theirs."

The alligator poked its head up on shore, and the four people stepped back hastily. They had no real fear of it, because they were better equipped to maneuver on the land. But it did seem that Man was now a minority species on the planet.

"We'll have to make a raft," Gus said. "Travel about, find others like us, start civilization over."

Zena, long on her feet, suddenly sat down on a mossy rock. "Oh-oh," Floy said. "Raft's going to have to wait."

"Look!" Gus cried, pointing across the water. "A boat!"

"Just let me rest," Zena said. "It's not due yet."

"Halloo!" Gus called, waving his hand in the air.

"Listen," Floy said, "I'm no expert, but I think it *is* due. We've got to get you back home."

Thatch's head turned back and forth. He didn't know whether to watch the boat or help Zena. But his decision was soon made. "A stretcher," he said. "We'll make a stretcher and carry you back."

"It's coming!" Gus exclaimed. "Two men."

"There's nothing to make a stretcher," Floy said. "We'll have to set up right here. See if there's a hot spring near."

"No." Zena protested futilely. "Not for another month!"

They made her as comfortable as possible, gathering soft moss to make a temporary bed. The contractions eased, then came again, harder. Zena knew it would happen long before a month had passed. She must have miscounted, after all.

Now the boat came near. It was a canoe, or rather a kayak, covered over with animal skins to seal out the water. The upper halves of two people showed, stroking with paddles on opposite sides so that the little craft glided smoothly and swiftly forward. A man and a woman, both young and vigorous.

"We'd better parlay with them before we go anywhere," Thatch said. "Maybe they can help."

But the boat stopped thirty feet from the shore, its occupants backpaddling to hold it in place. "We don't want any trouble," the man called. "You stay on your island, we'll stay on ours, okay?"

Gus and Thatch exchanged puzzled glances. "Trouble?"

Floy strode to the bank. "We have a woman in labor here. No drugs or anything. You're the first human beings we've seen since the second rain began. Please, help us!"

The kayak moved closer. "They *do!*" the woman said. "And we thought *we* had problems!"

"I don't see any weapons," the man said.

"Weapons!" Gus cried. "We don't want to fight! Too many people dead already."

"He has a scar," the man said.

The woman peered at Gus. "No, that's not the one."

"*I* put that scar on him, if you really want to know," Floy said. She showed her fingers. "But that was a personal matter. We don't want to—"

"We had to eat two of our own number just to get through," Gus said.

"Shut up!" Floy hissed, too late.

"You killed your own?" the man demanded suspiciously.

"No, of course not," Gus said. "One was killed when

185

bandits attacked us, just as the rain was starting. The other was a diabetic. We——" He broke off, remembering Karen. "What do you care, anyway? If you don't want to help——"

"Those bandits," the man said, showing interest. "Were they white or black?"

"White," Gus said. "One of them had a scar on his face. They came in with guns and knives, trying to take our home and women. We killed four. We don't have any decent home anymore, so there's nothing for you to take, if that's what you're——"

"Wait!" Zena cried, interrupting him. "They're black! That's why they distrust us!"

Gus did a double-take. "So they are! What difference does it make?"

"Those bandits," the man said. "They hit us a week before the second rain. Killed two men and a child, burned our house. We thought it was a race war. But if they went after you too——"

"You have children?" Floy asked.

"Three of them. Not ours; we're not a family. *Weren't*, anyway, before the rains. We had to eat our dead, too; there wasn't any other way, except the moss."

"Well, the bandits are dead," Gus said. "We found their camp."

"Zena and I worked over scarface," Floy said with relish. "And Dust Devil finished him off."

"We gave him that scar," the woman said.

"Any of you know nursing or medicine?" Floy asked. "We can't wait long."

"We have one old lady, used to be a midwife. You want to come in with us?"

"Sure," Gus said. "For now, anyway. See how it works out. We have a net for fishing, but it's hard to handle without plenty of manpower. Not much else we can contribute."

The boat pulled up to shore. "Okay," the man said.

"One of you came back with me, meet our people. Don't expect too much, at first—we're leary of whites, after what happened. But we'll make do, make a new start together. Joy'll stay here with you, talk things over. We'll fetch our midwife."

The pangs of labor were upon Zena again, but now she knew things were going to be all right. Joy was coming toward her solicitously, while Thatch struggled to enter the unfamiliar craft.

"Were you picked up in Florida?" Zena asked between spasms, remembering the girl they had lost.

"No. Never been there," Joy said.

Oh, well. Mankind would continue—and perhaps this time it would build on a better foundation.

# Afterword by Donald L. Cyr

The Annular Theory has been presented in this novel as
fiction. It is not. Isaac N. Vail was an obscure Quaker
scientist who lived from 1840 to 1912; he originated and
publicized this theory that there were once icy rings about
the Earth, similar to those now about the planet Saturn.
He suggested that these rings lost momentum, dropped
closer to our planet, and dissolved into a tremendous vapor canopy perhaps a hundred miles above the Earth's
surface. This vapor canopy could have been similar to
those of Jupiter and the other gas giants.

When sufficient material had been injected into this canopy, Vail suggests, it became unstable. As it spread out to
shroud all the planet, the portion near the north and south
poles had to fall. Vail believed that the lack of centrifugal
force toward the poles caused the downfall, but modern
interpretation considers that the interaction with Van Al-

len zones, whose impinging particles were discovered by space probes and earth satellites, could have been the controlling factor. Possibly future space probes that explore distant Jupiter may settle the issue of how such canopies operate. That the earth once had such a canopy that did fall in the poleward regions is at present still a viable scientific theory; all that remains is to settle the details.

Those details seem elusive. If we consider for the purposes of discussion that the Earth did have such a formation, similar to the cloud-banded formations on Jupiter and Saturn, we are faced with the question "Where do such canopies come from?" Various writers have taken different tacks at this point. Most astronomers consider that Jupiter's canopy is simply a surface phenomenon on that planet and, of course, they may be right about that. But until the mid 1940s, very few astronomers thought that Saturn's rings contained ice, and they were surprised when infrared evidence showed the presence of ice or frost-covered ring particles. To that extent, Vail's theories were vindicated—but a nagging question remains: Where does a ring system get its ice, and how can it remain stable? Again a set of alternatives is available to us. For Saturn, the answer is easy: ice rings are stable at that distance from the sun. For the Earth, the stability of a ring of ice leads to problems. Some scientists simply state that it would melt and disappear and so could not exist at all. Horbiger, an Austrian scientist, dealt with the problem in another way. He considered that either a lost Earth moon of ice had broken up, or perhaps an icy comet was captured by the Earth. Skipping over the stability problem for a moment, we may ask, "How much material is necessary to produce a canopy?" Again we have some alternatives or limits. If the ice from such a canopy produced *all* the ice of the last glacial epoch, for example, the amount would equal a layer of water over a hundred feet in depth over the entire earth. Since a cubic meter of water produces something like two million cubic meters of "fog," we would be calling for impossible dimensions for our hypothetical canopy. Fortunately, a very easy (and reasonable) alternative remains.

If we consider that a canopy had relatively little material, then we can invoke the phenomenon of "cloud seeding" to produce precipitation that would then provide glacial snows, thus piling up glaciation on the continents as is indicated in the records of geology. Incidentally, one theory under consideration by modern scientists considers that rainfall is sometimes initiated by meteoritic dust particles swept up from space by the Earth. A canopy that would collect particles for a time, and then collapse, might provide the kind of flooding and catastrophe that Piers Anthony has described in this novel.

Will a canopy formation ever return? Vail concluded that since the Earth now obviously has no ring system, there can never be another canopy. His very close friend, one Captain R. Kelso Carter, felt otherwise. Although Carter's reasoning is perhaps more mystical than scientific, he did feel that the Earth was destined to experience another canopy formation. For years, the writer of this summary agreed with Vail, that there simply was no source of material in space and no source of energy that would be capable of putting tons of water into orbit at the limits of the Earth's atmosphere. However, with the perfection of atomic energy, there is now a reasonable energy source. With new-found scientific skills, space scientists could provide a "little" canopy without much trouble at all. In fact, it appears more than ever that Captain R. Kelso Carter was correct. Indeed the canopy can return; the only ingredient missing now is the will to make it happen.

So whether the reinstatement of the canopy occurs by design, by space-scientist error, (or by Machiavellian plot), there may well be a return of the canopy. What then can you and I as ordinary citizens do about it? This novel suggests one response.

Man has experienced the fall of canopies in the past

and has survived them, according to Vail's interpretation of the records. Before ice epochs, man produced some of the most glorious works of art now found on cave walls, to tantalize and mystify us. Similarly, we can stand in awe before such monuments as Stonehenge, speculating that such structures might have been built during the peaceful days when a greenhouse-like canopy covered Britain and other parts of the world as well. This claim takes on new meaning inasmuch as halos appear to have influenced the design and arrangement of the Sarsen Stones of Stonehenge.

The arguments that show this latter conclusion are a little lengthy, and the reader is referred to a paper entitled "Stonehenge Evidence for Halo Phenomena," that was presented in June 1973 before the Astronomical Society of the Pacific. An abstract of this paper appears in the October, 1973, issue of *Publications* of the *Astronomical Society of the Pacific*. The article itself may be obtained by writing "Stonehenge Viewpoint," 25 W. Anapamu Street, Santa Barbara, Calif. 93101. There can be little doubt that much of the climatic analysis of the past would be well explained by a modest sized Vailian Canopy. To that extent, Piers Anthony's novel is less fiction than articulated fact. Perhaps his basic point is that whatever the environmental challenges, the interrelationships between humans will continue to be important. That idea too may be interpreted in fiction but is, inevitably, factual.

Donald L. Cyr